Murambi,
The Book
of Bones

Global African Voices

DOMINIC THOMAS, EDITOR

Murambi, The Book of Bones

Boubacar Boris Diop

TRANSLATED BY
Fiona Mc Laughlin

WITH A FOREWORD BY
Eileen Julien

Indiana University Press

BLOOMINGTON AND INDIANAPOLIS

This book is a publication of

Indiana University Press
Office of Scholarly Publishing
Herman B Wells Library 350
1320 East 10th Street
Bloomington, Indiana 47405 USA

iupress.indiana.edu

First Global African Voices edition 2016
Original publication in French © 2000 Boubacar Boris Diop/Editions Stock
English translation © 2006 by Indiana University Press
All rights reserved

Manufactured in the United States of America

The Library of Congress has cataloged the original edition as follows:

Diop, Boubacar Boris, 1946–
    [Murambi. English]
    Murambi : the book of bones / Boubacar Boris
        Diop ; translated by Fiona Mc Laughlin
    p. cm.
    Includes bibliographical references.
    ISBN 0-253-21852-7 (pbk.) — ISBN 0-253-34754-8 (cloth)
    1. Rwanda—History—Civil War, 1994—Fiction. 2. Genocide—
        Rwanda—Fiction. I. Mc Laughlin, Fiona. II. Title.
PQ3989.2.D553M8713 2006
843'.914—dc22

ISBN 978-0-253-34754-1 (cloth)
ISBN 978-0-253-21852-0 (pbk.)
ISBN 978-0-253-11206-4 (ebk.)
ISBN 978-0-253-02342-1 (pbk.)

1 2 3 4 5   21 20 19 18 17 16

For Mother
To El-Hadj Mama
and to Rina Mazor
—Boubacar Boris Diop

Contents

Foreword: An Urn for the Dead, an Hourglass for the Living

Eileen Julien

In April 2004, when the infamous photos from the Abu Ghraib prison in Iraq appeared in U.S. and international media, I was introducing my class's next reading assignment, a not-yet-published translation of *Murambi: The Book of Bones*, by Senegalese journalist and novelist Boubacar Boris Diop. *Murambi* had been written to bear witness to the Rwandan genocide. It was now the tenth anniversary of those horrific ninety days in which perhaps a million people or more were maimed and killed, as the world stood by. Abu Ghraib was remote from Murambi in its causes and effects, but the cruelty that was perpetrated at the prison and the headiness of those who had the power to be cruel to other human beings had been produced by similar processes of demonization. I knew that *Murambi* was a book we must read.

What does a novel such as this bring to the awful violence of genocide that journalistic accounts and histories cannot? These forms of narrative are held to a well-known standard of truth. They are meant to establish and report facts, to offer an accurate and balanced, if not objective, representation of events. *Murambi* does contain such elements. It makes plain that the slaughter was premeditated and prepared and that it had external support. But it does not delve into pre-colonial and colonial history to explain the shifting relations of domination that helped consolidate the divisive identities of Hutu, Tutsi, and Twa and fuel violent ethnic hatred. Nor does the novel propose the definitive and unambiguous answers we may be looking for—Why did the slaughter take place? What was the chronology? Who shall we blame?

Murambi's significance lies elsewhere. It does what a creative and transformative work alone can do. It distills this history and gives voice to those who can no longer speak—recovering, as best we can, the full, complex lives concealed in the statistics of genocide and rendering their humanity. In thinking about the gruesome murder of hundreds of thousands of people and this book—a frail object—we confront the enormous disproportion between the work of art, as beautiful and powerful as it may be, and the terrible events it symbolizes. Yet it is through the work of imagination and language that the novel reconstitutes those unique human beings, now lost to us, and allows them nonetheless to survive and to be heard. Their stories may lead us to reflect on the practice of evil and help us claim our very own humanity amidst the routine banality of violence, the numbed indifference or silent acquiescence of which we are all a part.

Murambi depicts and interweaves two moments: the atmosphere of menace as the genocide coalesces and unfolds and the aftermath in which Cornelius Uvimana, a Rwandan teacher who has lived abroad for twenty-five years, returns home to come to terms with this terrible history. The time, place, and mood of the genocide are created through a concert of voices. We readers simply "overhear" the thoughts of fictive victims and killers who lived through those terrifying and horrific days. We come away with a profound sense of the feelings that lay beneath the events—the "fear and anger," as Diop has entitled the opening section. Then, with Cornelius's return, his rediscovery of childhood friends and the reliving of their shared memories, his visit to his uncle Siméon Habineza and the school at Murambi—the site of a particularly gruesome massacre —the novel opens a space of reckoning, calling on us readers, like Cornelius, to reflect and weigh the question of responsibility, to imagine a new future.

Murambi obviously does not condone what the murderers did in the name of ethnic nationalism, yet it presents their voices plainly, without prejudice or indignation, affording no moral superiority to us who now observe in hindsight and from afar the unspeakable pain and loss of life. The novel's multiple voices are critical to a complex understanding of that time and place and the everyday logic of evil. We may read them also as a sign of the self-reproducing, never-ending spirals of violence; they intimate the complicated history that preceded the atrocities of 1994 and the ongoing repercussions of the genocide that continue to spill over Rwanda's borders.

Those ninety days in Rwanda are the focus of the novel, but in every sense the full story exceeds that frame, taking in us readers, too. Addressing a crowd of survivors, feverish to seek revenge, old Siméon insists: "You have suffered, but that doesn't make you any better than those who made you suffer. They are people like you and me. Evil is within each one of us. . . . you are not better than them." These remarks are directed toward Hutu and Tutsi survivors. But they are surely meant for us readers also. *Murambi* is indeed a cautionary tale, an African story with wide application: what happened in Rwanda in 1994—the scapegoating, the murderous objectifying of "the others"—could happen here or anywhere. In the twentieth century it has happened—in Germany, in Cambodia, in Bosnia. . . . But *Murambi* insists also that the Rwandan genocide is more than a "parable" for those on the other side of the world or continent. It is already and from its beginnings *our* story, a story that implicates the rest of us. For even as the novel and its characters grapple with Rwandan responsibility, *Murambi* also points a finger at those who looked the other way—because Africans have always been portrayed as hopeless and expendable, perennially consumed by ancient "tribal" hatreds.

One of the most haunting voices of *Murambi* belongs to Michel Serumundo, a Tutsi who will be slaughtered. He says in the opening pages of the novel:

> I've seen lots of scenes on television myself that were hard to take. Guys in slips and masks pulling bodies out of a mass grave. Newborns they toss, laughing, into bread ovens. Young women who coat their throats with oil before going to bed. "That way," they say, "when the throat-slitters come, the blades

of their knives won't hurt as much." I suffered from these things without really feeling involved. I didn't realize that if the victims shouted loud enough, it was so I would hear them, myself and thousands of other people on earth, and so we would try to do everything we could so that their suffering might end. It always happened so far away, in countries on the other side of the world. But in these early days of April in 1994, the country on the other side of the world is mine.

Mindful of the awful challenge and responsibility in writing this particular work, Boris Diop has expressed the hope that his work of fiction will not betray the suffering of the Rwandans who agreed to tell him of the horrible things they saw and through which they lived. Cornelius echoes that hope when he reaches the conviction in the final lines of the novel "that the dead of Murambi, too, had dreams, and that their most ardent desire was for the resurrection of the living." This quiet and stunning novel, the voices of *Murambi,* call on us as readers to fulfill that hope, to resist the temptation of complacency. *Murambi* leaves us with this question: How do we live responsibly in our violent world?

Acknowledgments

This translation was made possible by a fellowship from the National Endowment for the Humanities, and by the College of Liberal Arts and Sciences of the University of Florida and the Graduate School of the University of Kansas, whose generous support I gratefully acknowledge. I extend my sincere thanks to those who have in some way helped in bringing the translation to fruition, including Boubacar Boris Diop, Samba Gadjigo, Antoine Guillaume, Abdourahmane Idrissa, Eileen Julien, Bernth Lindfors, Mimi Mortimer, Carol Murphy, and Hal Wylie. I am especially grateful to Dee Mortensen at Indiana University Press and to Leonardo Villalón for having believed in the project from the very beginning.

Introduction: "To call a monster by its name"

Fiona Mc Laughlin

In 1998 a group of ten prominent African writers were invited to go on a two-month-long visit to post-genocide Rwanda to bear collective witness to one of the most horrifying tragedies of the twentieth century. The catalyst for this remarkable initiative was Nocky Djedanoum, Chadian journalist and writer, and co-director, with Maïmouna Coulibaly, of Fest'Africa, an annual African cultural festival in Lille, France. The startling literature that has come out of that expedition, which includes works by Monique Ilboudo of Burkina Faso, Tierno Monenembo from Guinea, and Ivoirian writer Véronique Tadjo, heralds a new commitment by writers in Africa to "call a monster by its name," a vow uttered by one of the central characters in *Murambi, The Book of Bones*. Manthia Diawara (2002) argues that this body of literature constitutes a turning point in African literature toward the reintegration of writers and intellectuals into the public sphere of political engagement within the continent, rather than from the vantage point of exile in the West. "With the Rwandan Expedition," he writes, "one dares to dream of a renewed life and space for African literature. After slavery and colonialism, disease and human rights violations are some of the most important crises facing Africa today. The intellectuals' role in the public sphere is crucial to denouncing such violations and arguing for democracy and tolerance" (2002: 15). Boubacar Boris Diop's fifth novel, *Murambi*, is part of this new literature of *engagement.* In recognition of its literary and political value *Murambi* was included in the Zimbabwe International Book Fair's list of the one hundred most important African books of the twentieth century, a list compiled at the millennium.

Murambi's most immediate importance lies, obviously, in its subject matter, namely the overwhelming tragedy of the Rwandan genocide. In April of 1994, as he was returning from peace talks in Arusha, Tanzania, Rwandan president Juvénal Habyarimana's plane was shot down while preparing to land in the Kigali airport, killing the president and all others who were on board. The world stood by in disbelief at what ensued: the massacre of hundreds of thousands of men, women, and children, predominantly of Tutsi ethnicity—the official figures count 800,000 deaths, but how accurate they are, no one knows—most of whom were hacked to death with machetes and knives. In a chilling commentary on the genocide, which ran a course of one hundred days, Samantha Power writes, "The Rwandan genocide would prove to be the fastest, most efficient killing spree of the twentieth century" (2002: 334). The Rwandan genocide of 1994 was clearly a world tragedy, not only an African tragedy. Its specter continues to haunt not only the central African political and social landscape, but the rest of the world as well. In particular, it raises uncomfortable questions about intervention by Western countries that failed to act to help prevent the bloodshed, a scenario that is being relived as similar events unfold in the Darfur region of Sudan.

Boubacar Boris Diop is one of Africa's very best contemporary novelists. His works have won major literary prizes, including the Prix de la République du Sénégal, the Prix Tropiques, and most recently the Grand Prix Littéraire d'Afrique Noire. A public intellectual and political activist who was once a high school philosophy teacher, he is also a journalist and one of the founding editors of *Sud*, Senegal's first independent newspaper, dubbed "the newspaper of the people" by one of the characters in the late Senegalese cinematographer Djibril Diop Mambety's film *La Petite vendeuse de Soleil*. In addition to *Murambi*, Diop's novels include *Le Temps de Tamango* (1981), *Les Tambours de la mémoire* (1990), *Les Traces de la meute* (1993), and *Le Cavalier et son ombre* (1997) as well as a (2003) novel written in Wolof, *Doomi golo*. All deal in an iconoclastic way with myth and history and what they mean to Africans living in the present, but as Sugnet (2001: 142) points out, Diop's myths are essentially inconclusive, appearing as fragments, interpreted in a multiplicity of ways and by a multiplicity of narrators. In the shadow of genocide, where the identity of an individual is subjugated to a nebulous collective category such as Tutsi or Hutu, the most human response is to seek the uniqueness of individual experience and memory, to tell the individual's story. *Murambi* is first and foremost a novel of individual narratives, resembling Diop's previous polyphonic novels in the multiplicity of narrative voices it employs. Chapters bear the names of their narrators, a litany of witnesses, perpetrators, victims, and onlookers. It is through these individual accounts that the atrocities of the genocide are revealed, from the initial fear and disbelief on the day that Habyarimana's plane is shot down, to the horrifying and often relentless details of the massacres and tortures, to the reflection that goes on afterwards in the minds of the survivors.

Diop's double career as a journalist and a novelist works its way into *Murambi* in profound ways. As a journalist, the author is both fascinated and horrified by the role that the media played in the Rwandan genocide. While soccer matches keep the rest of the world entertained, in Rwanda the radio takes on a most sinister role. The infamous Radio Mille Collines punctuates the novel with incendiary messages of hatred, goading people to murder. Call-in game shows make jokes about how to recognize a Tutsi, and when the first French troops arrive the announcer tells Hutu women, "make yourselves pretty, the French soldiers are here, now's your chance, because all the Tutsi girls are dead!" What is truly horrifying here is the way in which the genocide is rendered banal and packaged within the norms of the medium as entertainment, until its seduction gives way to the sobering realization that genocide ought not to be the stuff of game shows, and that the disembodied voice of Radio Mille Collines is itself an actor in the genocide.

As one of the first fictional accounts of the Rwandan genocide, Diop's novel grapples with how to translate the horrific events that occurred in 1994 into literature in a responsible manner. His conviction that literature is the ideal medium for translating the genocide was only arrived at after much soul searching, and a large part of the novel is devoted to a dialogue about literature and responsibility, carried out through the development of the central character, Cornelius Uvimana, who, like Diop, is a writer. Also like Diop, Cornelius was not in Rwanda during the genocide, but has come back to Rwanda four years later to try to come to terms with history and to write a play about the genocide, ignorant of the fact that his father was directly responsible for the massacre of thousands of people who were taking refuge in a school in the northern town of Murambi. As a writer, Cornelius is frequently embarrassed by his profession when it is juxtaposed against the gravity of the genocide, and he struggles with the responsibility of turning such subject matter into fiction. One night, as he wanders drunk through the streets of Kigali with a friend, he recounts part of a grotesque play he will write on the genocide. The play, which involves an Ubu-like French general who has his agents "torture, rape, and kill" in order to find his cat who has disappeared during the genocide, is literature gone wrong. Cornelius is warned many times that literature cannot carry the unbearable weight of the genocide. Gérard, a man who drank blood to escape being killed in the Murambi massacre, tells him, "all the beautiful words of the poets, Cornelius, can say nothing, I swear to you, of the fifty thousand ways to die like a dog." But although he is ashamed of his attempt at writing a play, Cornelius refuses to be silent, and eventually decides that his responsibility as a writer is "to call a monster by its name." At this point the reader understands why the graphic and disturbing details of the genocide have been told again and again until we are worn down by them. Neither Cornelius Uvimana nor Boris Diop has given up on literature.

NOTE

Some passages of this essay were previously published in Mc Laughlin (2002). I am grateful to Africa World Press for permission to reproduce them here.

SOURCES

Diawara, Manthia. 2002. "African literature and the Rwandan expedition." Unpublished manuscript, New York University.

Diop, Boubacar Boris. 1997. *Le Cavalier et son ombre.* Paris: Stock.

———. 2003. *Doomi golo.* Dakar: Papyrus.

———. 2000. *Murambi, le livre des ossements.* Paris: Stock.

———. 1990. *Les Tambours de la mémoire.* Paris: L'Harmattan.

———. 1981. *Le Temps de Tamango.* Paris: L'Harmattan.

———. 1993. *Les Traces de la meute.* Paris: L'Harmattan.

Mambety, Djibril Diop. 1999. *La petite vendeuse de Soleil.* (Film.)

Mc Laughlin, Fiona. 2002. "Writing the Rwandan Genocide: Boubacar Boris Diop's *Murambi, le livre des ossements.*" In Toyin Falola and Barbara Harlow, eds., *Palavers of African Literature: Essays in Honor of Bernth Lindfors.* Vol. 1, pp. 203–220. Trenton, N.J., and Asmara, Eritrea: Africa World Press.

Power, Samantha. 2002. *"A Problem from Hell": America and the Age of Genocide.* New York: HarperCollins.

Sugnet, Charles J. 2001. "Dances with Wolofs: A Conversation with Boubacar Boris Diop." *Transition* 10(3):138–159.

Murambi,
The Book
of Bones

PART ONE | *Fear*

and

Anger

Michel Serumundo

Yesterday I stayed at the video shop a bit later than usual. Granted, there hadn't been many customers during the day, which is rather surprising for this time of month. To keep myself busy I set about organizing the films on the shelves in the hopes that someone would come and rent one at the last minute. Then I went and stood at the doorway to the shop for a few minutes. People were passing by without stopping.

This corner of the Kigali market where I set up shop nine years ago appeals to me less and less. Back then we all knew each other. Our shops formed a little circle near the crossroads. When customers were scarce, we could at least get together over a beer among friends to complain about the hard times. But unfortunately, over the course of several months, all sorts of people—tailors, vegetable and cloth sellers, butchers and barbers—had taken possession of the tiniest bit of sidewalk. The result was a colorful and friendly chaos, but it wasn't necessarily good for business.

By half past nine I really had to go home to Nyaka-banda, almost without a penny in my pocket. On the way to the bus station I heard sirens roaring and I thought that there must have been another fire in one of the poorer neighborhoods of the city.

A tank from the presidential guard unit had taken up position at the entrance to the station. One of three soldiers in combat gear asked me politely for my identity card. While he was leaning over to read it I followed his gaze. Sure enough, the first thing they want to know is whether you're supposed to be Hutu, Tutsi, or Twa.

"Ah, Tutsi . . . " he said, staring me in the eye.

"That's what it says, doesn't it?" I answered with a smirk.

He appeared to hesitate a bit, then gave me back my card, shaking his head. Just as I was about to leave, grumbling to myself, a second soldier called me back. He seemed to be much less accommodating than his colleague. He pointed to my trousers and said harshly:

"First, see to your fly, my friend."

I fixed it, smiling stupidly. I must have had a sly look.

"Oh! Thank you. I hadn't noticed."

"You work in this market?"

"What a moron!" I thought.

"If I didn't work in this market do you think I'd come here to get a bus?"

I had spoken curtly, to show him just how stupid I found his question.

"Where do you work then?"

This guy was too much. Why this "then"? I almost asked him, but he didn't seem to be joking at all.

"I am Michel Serumundo, owner of the Fontana video shop," I replied, trying to sound modest.

In spite of my visible irritation, my sense of business had quickly gotten the better of me. I told him that I specialized in renting out war films. After all, soldiers must love to watch bombings, ambushes, and all that kind of thing. Was I going to tell him about those special adult films too? I decided not to. He gave me back my identity card. It was clear something was eating him.

Patting me on the shoulder, he signaled to me to leave. "That's fine, go on."

It dawned on me later that he had taken me for a madman. As I moved away I felt them staring at me, baffled. I wondered what they could be doing at the entrance to the market at this time of night. The question ran through my head for a few moments. It's true that this part of the Kigali market almost always draws a large crowd. So naturally it attracts bombers like those who made two attacks last March, one of which killed five people. But I don't remember having seen any soldiers in this place other than during rush hour. What could their presence mean? Maybe they had some other information. I thought again of the roaring sirens and started to feel slightly uneasy.

The market bus station was almost deserted. I climbed onto the only vehicle parked there. The atmosphere was heavy inside the bus, and the passengers sat in silence. After a few minutes, the driver called his apprentice.

"OK. Let's go."

It was only when a group of nervous soldiers stopped our bus from passing in front of Radio Rwanda that I started to suspect that this was a day unlike any other.

The driver, who was going at a very brisk pace, had to

stop dead in front of the roadblock. Instantly, soldiers appeared from every direction with crazed eyes. The idiots were really ready to shoot at us. They asked the driver for his papers and one of them shone his flashlight in our faces. He lingered on mine for a long time and I thought he was going to make me get out.

The other one was harsh on the driver:

"Hey, didn't you see the roadblock?"

"I'm sorry, sir."

The driver was shitting in his pants. His voiced was trembling.

We made a U-turn and a big man with a mustache, wearing a blue jacket, blurted out in a loud and almost joyful voice:

"This time they're not joking, are they?"

I waited, but he didn't say anything else. "What's going on?" I asked.

The guy glared at me. All of a sudden he seemed to be furious with me.

"That's it," he said coldly without taking his eyes off me, "they're going to tell us again that it's an unfortunate accident."

I tried to look inconspicuous in my corner. Most of the passengers agreed with the man and repeated that this time it wasn't going to happen that way. They said it was going to be a field day for the militia. My blood froze. The Interahamwe militia, whose only purpose in life was to kill Tutsis. Someone announced that he had seen a ball of fire fall from the sky.

"It's a sign from God," the man in the blue suit assured us.

"Did you know that the plane fell on the lawn in his garden?"

"On the lawn?"

"In his garden?"

"Yes, in his house!"

"That's a sure sign from God."

"God loved that man! All the heads of state in the world respected him."

"They were jealous," added another. "President Mitterrand gave him a plane as a gift and they said: 'Since we can't have one of our own, we're going to destroy it!'"

I was apparently the only one who didn't know that our president Juvénal Habyarimana's plane had just been shot down in full flight by two missiles on that day, Wednesday, April 6th, 1994.

My heart began to beat very fast and I felt a mad desire to talk to someone. I turned toward my neighbor on the left who hadn't opened his mouth once. He held a young girl of five or six on his lap. She was lovely in her dress of scarlet flowers. The man was crying quietly. Was it Habyarimana's death that had made him so sad? It wasn't impossible, but then again, it would have surprised me. People don't generally cry for their president unless the television is there to film them. It's true, these African presidents give people such a hard time, they shouldn't delude themselves. It makes complete sense. Nevertheless, the unknown man had touched me enormously. While he was forcing himself in vain to hold back his tears the little girl played with him, sticking a bird feather in his ear, and her clear little laugh resounded through the bus.

When we had passed the dispensary—I think it's called the Good Samaritan—the driver took a right-hand turn and said sullenly as he was parking, "Everyone gets off here."

"What about my luggage?" protested a woman who had a heavy basket beside her.

"Motor's broken," said the driver curtly.

I called him a bastard, but he just kept staring straight ahead. He was lying through his teeth. Then, addressing his apprentice, he spat out grudgingly, "Hey, give them back their money."

He had been dying of fright ever since the incident in front of Radio Rwanda, and most likely he thought that the easiest thing to do was to go home. The presidential guard and the gendarmerie were all over the place with their cars and beacons and the screaming of their sirens. It was like a city under siege.

I had to do three kilometers on foot to get back to my house in Nyakabanda. Groups of young people bustled about, blocking the big avenues and the entrances to each neighborhood with tree trunks, tires, rocks, and burnt-out cars. You could also see some more ordinary barricades made from simple iron grating. They did things seriously, with a sinister concentration and without too much fuss, lit by the glow of their flashlights. Sometimes they argued heatedly about the placement of a barricade. Their leader would arrive quickly to give orders and everyone would go back to work.

In spite of the late hour, Séraphine was waiting for me at the doorway to the house, her face serious.

"Where are the children?" I said.

"Only Pierrot's missing."

Him again. There were always problems with that scatterbrain of a Jean-Pierre.

"I'm going to look for him."

"Where?" asked Séraphine. "The radio just announced that everyone should stay at home."

That didn't make any sense. I couldn't let my twelve-year-old son spend the night away from home at a time like this. Whoever knew Rwanda knew terrible things were going to happen.

"And is everything alright here?" I asked, gesturing toward the house with my chin.

We lived with a Hutu family. They were polite, but their son, a fanatical Interahamwe militiaman, was often nasty to us. One day I caught him going through our things. I closed the door and said, "Defend yourself, kid." He likes to play the tough guy to impress the girls in the neighborhood, but he doesn't know how to fight. He got a thrashing he'll never forget. Anyway, I supposed he must have been remembering all about it during these last few hours. Yes, the time has come for them to settle all those little scores. Every Interahamwe probably has his list of little Tutsi friends to get rid of.

"The neighbors? They haven't said a word to me all evening," said Séraphine.

"And our young imbecile, is he there?"

"Don't shout, Michel, please. He's disappeared."

My guess was that he was with the others, putting up barricades at all the crossroads in the city.

Séraphine wanted to say something, but she held back at the last moment.

The situation was becoming clearer and clearer, but I didn't want to make her any more worried.

"Don't worry, Séra, the entire world is watching them, they won't be able to do anything."

"You think so?"

"Of course."

In my heart of hearts I knew I was wrong. The World Cup was about to begin in the United States. The planet was interested in nothing else. And in any case, whatever happened in Rwanda, it would always be the same old story of blacks beating up on each other. Even Africans would say, during half-time of every match, "They're embarrassing us, they should stop killing each other like that." Then they'll go on to something else. "Did you see that acrobatic flip of Kluivert's?" What I'm saying is not a reproach. I've seen lots of scenes on television myself that were hard to take. Guys in slips and masks pulling bodies out of a mass grave. Newborns they toss, laughing, into bread ovens. Young women who coat their throats with oil before going to bed. "That way," they say, "when the throat-slitters come, the blades of their knives won't hurt as much." I suffered from these things without really feeling involved. I didn't realize that if the victims shouted loud enough, it was so I would hear them, myself and thousands of other people on earth, and so we would try to do everything we could so that their suffering might end. It always happened so far away, in countries on the other side of the world. But in these early days of April in 1994, the country on the other side of the world is mine.

My conversation with Séraphine took place in the street. "Go in for a few minutes at least," she said to me. "The children will be happy to see you."

"They haven't gone to bed yet? It's eleven o'clock at night."

"The teacher told them that there won't be any class tomorrow. So . . . "

"OK, I'll go and tease them a bit."

I had just realized that our house now, all of a sudden, seemed to frighten us. I went inside. Our neighbors' shutters were hermetically sealed. They were listening to Radio Mille Collines, the station which for several months now has been issuing insane calls to murder. That was new. Up to now they had been listening to those stupid programs in secret. I found the children in the living room. While I was playing with them, I remembered the man crying silently on the bus. Then I sprang up to go in search of Jean-Pierre. I also intended to stop by the storage room to lock up some valuable things that people had given to me to look after. The looting could start at any moment. Looting, and one or two thousand dead, that would almost be the least evil. I'm not exaggerating. This country has been completely mad for a long time. In any case, this time the murderers had the perfect excuse: the death of the president. I didn't dare to hope that they would be satisfied with just a little blood.

Faustin
Gasana

I sat down beside the driver. He started the engine and asked in his usual laconic way:

"Where to, boss?"

"We'll stop by the house, Danny. The old man is anxious to talk to me."

He sets off in a cloud of dust. In normal times the traffic is very heavy in this part of Kibungo. This afternoon the streets are deserted. The inhabitants have been cloistered away at home for two days. The only people moving around are security forces and Interahamwe militia like me. I sense a discreet excitement in Danny. I haven't told him anything about it, but he knows that some very important events are going to take place. For twenty-four hours he's been driving me from one meeting to another. Besides, last night I had to tell him to go home without me since it was clear that our meeting with the prefects and mayors was not going to end before dawn.

I pushed open the door of the house. My sister Hortense is frying plantain bananas in the open-air kitchen, just to the left of the entranceway.

"Hello, little sister."

She comes toward me and whispers gaily into my ear with the face of a plotter:

"Go quickly and answer the old man. But I'm warning you: he's angry at you."

"I was very busy. Can't he understand that?"

"You know him. He says you're a bad son."

As soon as she hears my voice, Mother comes out of the old man's room. We run in to each other in the courtyard. She is holding a little tray. Some pieces of cotton float on a mixture of pus, blood, and alcohol.

"I've just changed his bandages," she says.

"Is the cut on his arm getting any better?"

Mother is quiet for a moment. She is not very talkative, and maybe she doesn't want to reply. Finally, she shakes her head, no.

"Come on." I said. "We're going to make him see a doctor."

"He chased me out of his room. He says you have to have a man-to-man talk."

I lower my eyes. The old man has always been very hard on her. Nevertheless, even if she suffers because of it, she never lets it show.

After pulling aside the curtain I have to wait for a few seconds at the threshold, just long enough for my eyes to get used to the darkness of the room. Like all old people's rooms, this one is cluttered with useless objects that make it even more cramped and stifling. Two photos are stuck on the wall, just above the headboard. In one of them, Grégoire Kayibanda, the first president of Rwanda, is shaking hands with King Baudouin of Belgium. Kayibanda seems very proud to be living this historic moment, and the king of the Belgians, white-gloved, seems a little distracted or disdainful. The other is the official portrait of Major-General Juvénal Habyarimana. The very man that our enemies have just murdered. He is smiling, and his eyes sparkle with intelligence.

My father is sitting in the middle of the bed. The transistor radio beside him exudes doleful music. His eyes can hardly see any more, but he senses my presence and holds out both his hands to me. I take them, trying to avoid re-awakening his pain. The same yellowish liquid seeps out from the white bandage wound around his left arm. It stinks a bit. So robust only a few years ago, he is at present thin, fragile, and rather shriveled. He turns off the radio and has me sit down on the bed, almost completely against him. I am touched by this gesture of affectionate complicity.

Father asks me straight away:

"Do those people take us for real men or for women?"

Without leaving me the time to respond he adds that this time, "'They' have gone too far."

Politics has always been his favorite topic of conversation, but I have never heard him pronounce the word "Tutsi." He always calls them "them" or "Inyenzi," literally cockroaches.

"We'll teach them to respect us," I say after a moment of reflection. "We're ready."

"I know you're doing good things for your country. Friends have come to congratulate me. I'm pleased with you."

"Yes, I've done good work. I know. We have the situation well in hand in the hills and in all the big cities in the country, but in the north it will be more difficult."

"Because of the Mulindi-based guerrillas?"

"Yes. We've heard that they've been moving on Kigali since Friday."

"That's what I'm told too."

"You're decidedly well informed," I say, smiling.

Flattered, he smiles too, then, suddenly becoming serious again, "You cannot fail."

His comment makes me ill at ease. After all, he's right. Despite his physical decrepitude, the old man has kept an amazingly quick mind. It's true, if we don't succeed in eliminating all the Tutsi, we'll be considered the bad guys in this business. They'll trot out their sob stories before the entire world and things will get very complicated for us. Even the most reluctant among us know it: after the first machete blow, we'll have to see it through to the bitter end.

"I don't know, Father. I can very well tell you, it's not going to be easy to manage both the war against the RPF, and everything else."

"Everything else?" he starts again with a scornful air. "Don't start off by being ashamed of what's in store for you."

I have the awful impression that he has doubts about my commitment. I am not so much offended as disappointed, because I want to speak to him openly.

He shouts, and I get a whiff of his bad breath right in my face. I shrink back a bit.

I repeat: "It'll be difficult."

"How well do you know the story of these Inyenzi Rwandan Patriotic Front guerrillas?"

It's the kind of question he always asks when he's about to recount one of his numerous anecdotes.

"I've learned some things about the RPF," I answer prudently.

"And do you know how their leader escaped death in 1961?"

"No," I admit, recoiling again.

I'm finding it harder and harder to stand his bad breath. Granted, things aren't going very well in his stomach either. His intestines have been giving him terrible trouble since his three-week stay last year with our relatives from Cyangugu.

"Well, it was at Gitarama, where we Hutus were the strongest. While our people were busy looting and raping, a four-year-old child and his parents were waiting for a car in order to escape toward Mutara. Suddenly, our men saw the Inyenzi family hurrying to get into the car. They ran after them. But it was too late. That's how those imbeciles, thirty-seven years ago, let the kid who is now the head of the guerrilla force escape."

Actually, I know this story well. I just don't want to deprive the old man of the pleasure of telling it to me. I could even tell him that the incident happened on Nyarutovu Hill, in the town of Ntambwe. We've heard it thousands of times from the mouths of our trainers. It's the example they always gave us to show us how dangerous it can be to spare babies during our work. Besides, the tale has numerous variations. In one version, the boy supposedly relents and even makes our guys laugh by swearing to them, "I won't ever be a Tutsi again." They also say that right when our bus was taking off, someone noticed the child and signaled to the driver to stop. But the driver supposedly refused to waste his time on a tiny little kid. Each version has its own partisans. One of our trainers joked about the fact that the kid from Nyarutovu hadn't kept his promise, but that that was predictable for an Inyenzi. On the contrary, he became our most dangerous enemy and took an evil pleasure in killing as many Hutus as he could. The trainer—his name was Léonard Majyambere—went through the ranks and asked what conclusion a good Interahamwe man should draw from all that. Even the dunces knew the answer.

"The most important thing," declares the old man, "wasn't to have killed the child. . . . "

I look at him carefully. What is he getting at?

"They were supposed to let him live? You're always saying that a brave man should see things through to the end."

"Of course," says the old man "they should have eliminated him. But the problem wouldn't even have come up if instead of getting drunk and looting our men had concentrated on their work. Explain it carefully to those who are under your command, that kind of behavior is a waste of their time and energy."

I think to myself that the old man has no sense of reality anymore.

"Of course, father. I'm going to insist upon discipline."

He notices immediately that I'm not taking his advice seriously and that I just want to avoid the discussion. He misses nothing. He unleashes spitefully:

"Do what you want, but since 1959 we've been making the same mistakes."

Things are starting to go wrong. I keep quiet. But it takes more than that to dishearten the old man.

"Surely you've heard of the Frenchman who wanted to kill all the white Inyenzi during their big war there. . . . "

"He was a German."

"What was his name?"

I feel a bit annoyed. I've never liked his odd habit of asking questions that, in many cases, he often already knows the answers to.

"Hitler."

"Hitler what?" he insists, studying me with his malicious eyes.

"Adolf. Adolf Hitler. They called him the Führer," I added, in order to preempt the next question.

"So tell me: Did he succeed in eliminating all the white Inyenzi?"

I refuse to go there. I've had enough of his drivel. All this time wasted. . . .

I say, "We'll talk about it again some other time. I have to go."

Very angry, he shouts:

"That white man was much better organized than you but he failed. You're nothing but a pretentious little bunch of idiots!"

I get up.

"Work's waiting for me," I say, trying to appear calm.

"You're mad aren't you? How dare you get mad at your father?"

"Don't be angry. I have to go because we're starting tonight here in Kibungo."

He replies calmly.

"Go away. You're a generation of incompetents."

He has lowered his voice to put into it all the force he can muster, which makes his words sound even more terrible.

I'm fond of the old man. He's my father. But he's like all those old people who discover miraculous answers to the world's problems on their deathbed. Things aren't so simple. I've always known in becoming an Interahamwe that I might well have to kill people myself or perish under their blows. That's never been a problem for me. I've studied the history of my country and I know that the Tutsis and us, we could never live together. Never. Lots of shirkers claim otherwise, but I don't believe it. I'm going to do my work properly. And I agree with the old man: every time you hurl insults at someone who's about to die, you give someone else the time to escape. I'm not so stupid that I can't see that. But how do I get that into my men's heads? They joined the Interahamwe militia to make men and women more powerful than them tremble. They look down on the idea of killing all the Tutsis. They would just as soon let some of them escape for the pleasure of future revenges just as bloody.

As I take leave of the old man—he doesn't even deign to take the hand I offer to him—strange ideas begin to assail me. Only words whose meaning remained obscure to me at the time. To think the unthinkable. My father's fetid breath. A father who can't finish dying. Always cursing and chasing someone out of his house. And all those Tutsis to kill. I didn't think there were so many of them. I have the feeling that the planet is inhabited by Tutsis. That we are the only people in the world who aren't Tutsis. Before, it was so easy to yell out like thunder, "*Tubatsembatsembe!*" We have to kill them all!

In the courtyard, I find my sisters and some neighbors seated around my mother. I take a seat in a chair and Louise offers me a glass of tea.

Mother scolds her. "Put a bit of mint in it. You know that Faustin only likes tea with mint."

We talk about this and that. I've never seen people so tense. In these hours of incertitude it's everyone for himself. They want to know more about it, but I avoid any allusion to the events. The only one who remains serene is my mother. Once again, I can't read anything in her face. That's what makes her unique in the world. No one has ever been able to get inside her head. But all the same, it's clear, she's always thinking about lots of things. Her mental strength is extraordinary. Today there is no way of knowing whether she approves of what is about to happen or not. Maybe she considers us all monsters? While I'm wondering about this, my sisters and the neighbors are eyeing me intently. Louise, the youngest one, is especially proud because her fiancé, Adrien, is part of my group. I have the sensation of reliving a scene from ancient times, from times when the bravery of warriors was exalted before battle. To be frank, I am by nature rather reserved, and all of that rather bothers me. I am not going to war. I am not running any risk. In Kibungo, like in the rest of Rwanda, we're just going to line the Tutsis up along the barricades and kill them. Each one in turn. Lots of them are taking refuge in churches and public buildings. They think they'll be able to get out of it, like before, during my father's time. That's the most serious mistake they've made in a long time. On the contrary, they'll make the job easier for us. To kill so many defenseless people will surely cause us some problems. In the long run it can be monotonous and wearisome. The old man is wrong. No one will be able to stop our boys from drinking, from singing and dancing to give themselves the courage for their work.

I have to insist a bit for them to agree to let me leave. The emotional farewells go on and on. The neighbors advise me to be careful and my sisters have trouble hiding their feelings.

As for my mother, she remains silent. At no moment do our eyes meet.

I don't know which one of us is avoiding the other's look.

As I open the door of the car I see heads peeping out

above the fences of the neighboring houses. My brand new company Pajero must impress a lot of people in this poor neighborhood where I was born. It's easy to guess from their avid stares that people are saying to themselves, "He's made it, old Casimir Gatabazi's son! He's really someone now, little Faustin!" I won't be hypocritical: I'm pleased by it. It's always intoxicating to read the proof of one's own success in other people's eyes.

"Where to?" says Danny again.

I look at my watch.

"Maybe I have enough time left to go and give Marie-Hélène a kiss before getting back to headquarters, Danny. I don't know when I'll see her again. She's bound to be angry, her too."

Danny smiled with a knowing glance.

"Ah, Marie-Hélène. Now there's a good woman!"

He's said it to please me because he knows that I'm madly in love with Marie-Hélène.

"I'm sorry for staying in there so long, Danny. I have a very strange father."

"Ah, Papa, he's very good too!"

Now I'm sure he doesn't mean a word of it. Danny knows all about the investigation he's been carrying out on him. The old man suspected him—without any reason whatsoever—of being a secret Inyenzi, charged by our RPF enemies with getting rid of me at the appointed time.

At bridge height, on the Kibungo market road, the soldiers of the presidential guard recognize me. I give them a friendly wave without stopping.

Next we pass in front of the restaurant Le Royal and I remember that I've hardly eaten anything since yesterday. I ask Danny to turn around.

The Royal is empty. Alphonse Ngarambe, the Tutsi owner, is busy talking with two of his employees. He is quiet when he sees me come in. After greeting them in the most natural way in the world I settle in near the window in the back. It's Marie-Hélène's and my favorite place. Alphonse knows me well, but considering the circumstances, he can't really welcome me with the same jovial familiarity as on other days. There is hardly anything to eat in his kitchen. But Alphonse goes to great lengths to fry me up a bit of fish and cassava. He, like so many others, is living the most terrifying hours of his life. When he serves me, his entire body trembles. I pretend to be absorbed in a foreign fashion magazine that's lying around. The effort that Alphonse is making to hide his fear from me is making him more and more agitated. He won't let me pay, but I insist. Then he puts on that lame smile that I find annoying. I hurry out of the restaurant.

I go by Marie-Hélène's. She doesn't make a scene. On the contrary, she understands perfectly well, she says, that the country is living a decisive moment. She just alludes to the stories of rape. It's true that they're talking a lot about it. The youngest ones are very excited by the idea that they'll be able to have sex with young women any time they want, just like that. They've always been told that the path to intimacy with a woman is long, complex, and often discouraging. They're discovering with pleasure that times can change very quickly. Marie-Hélène doesn't want me to get mixed up in all that. I promised her, but not without thinking, "To each his own problems."

Back at headquarters my men's joyful cheers welcome me.

We're sure to be keeping watch until very late. Contrary to what I told the old man, it's tomorrow that the serious business begins for us. All night long we'll play with our machetes, like swords, to the cry of *Tubatsembatsembe!*"

The game involves raising our machetes toward the sky and scraping them one against the other. It's fun, all this noise and all these sparks, and besides, we're sharpening the blades. At least that's what my boys believe. I'm not as sure about it as all that, but I let them do it.

| Jessica

"They love each other like crazy, those two. And now events are forcing them to postpone the date of their marriage again!"

"Ah! Lucienne and her boyfriend Valence Ndimbati . . . It's so sad," I say distractedly.

You get used to anything very fast. In her hometown of Nyamata where my friend Theresa Mukandori is looking for a refuge, we find a way to chatter on like two old women. She asks me suddenly, stopping,

"Do you really think they're going to do it?"

I've learned to lie.

"It's impossible, Theresa. They're looking mainly to scare people. It'll calm down in a few days."

The idea that from now on she could be killed at any moment by anybody seemed very odd to her.

As for me, I lead a double life. There are things that I can't talk about to anyone. Not even to Theresa. For example, this message dated April 8, 1994, that I've just received from Bisesero. Stéphane Nkubito, our comrade in that district, wrote it a few hours before being discovered and slaughtered. It seems to me that they didn't take the time to question him. They suspected that he was a member of the Rwandan Patriotic Front, operating in Bisesero. The letter from our comrade shows just how organized and determined the killers are. They're really ready to go all out this time around.

Stéphane tells me that on Thursday, April 7, 1994, Abel Mujawamarya, a businessman from Kigali, arrived in Gisovu with two yellow trucks full of machetes. He had them unloaded at the home of Olivier Bishirandora. The latter, who has a forge in his workshop, immediately started sharpening the machetes. Olivier, a member of Parmehutu/DRM was also the mayor of Gisovu in the seventies, during the time of President Kayibanda.

Abel Mujawamarya then organized a meeting, during which he gave out machetes and grenades to the Hutus. The Interahamwe then started to terrorize the Tutsis, accusing them of having murdered their beloved president, Juvénal Habyarimana. They set to, looting and setting fire to the Tutsis' houses, and then killed some of them. The Tutsis started fleeing their houses to take refuge in the parish churches of Mubaga and Kibingo, as well as in the Mugonero hospital. Others preferred to head for the mountains.

Stéphane Nkubito asks me to make a note and spread the word that the inhabitants of Bisesero, those tough warriors, intend to put up a fight. Since 1959, every time there are massacres, they get organized and at least succeed in driving back their attackers. At times they've even been able to get back their stolen animals through bold punitive expeditions. That's why, adds Stéphane, their reputation for being invincible is circulating around Rwanda. Refugees are flocking in from all over the place. But between the lines of his letter, Stéphane's fears were clear: according to his sources, the government is intending to put an end to the myth of invincibility of the Abasero, as the Tutsis of the Bisesero region are called. The army will do the bulk of the work, and Interahamwe militia reinforcements will be dispatched from Gisenyi and other towns where, because of the relatively small number of Tutsis among their populations, the massacres will be over earlier than elsewhere.

I read and reread Stéphane's message. At the bottom of the page there's a little drawing with the following caption: "Jessica Kamanzi making the victory sign."

Jessica Kamanzi, that's me. I smile as I look at my two fingers raised triumphantly toward the sky. Oh yes, victory is certain. I've never doubted it, not even for a moment. But it will be so bitter. . . .

I'd love to keep the drawing as a memento of Stéphane Nkubito. I finally decide to give it up: my comrade thinks he's being watched. I tear the message into pieces.

Theresa touches my arm:

"This is it," she says in a low voice.

We're in the neighborhood of the parish church of Nyamata, right near the lodgings of the Salesian Fathers who people say are originally from Brazil. Behind the thick curtain of eucalyptus and acacia, we can see people hurrying by the hundreds into the church.

"I'm going," says Theresa. "You'd better come with me, Jessica."

I think the exact opposite. The fighters I came with into Kigali found out that future victims were being encouraged to take refuge in the churches so that they could be exterminated there. But I have nothing else to propose to Theresa.

"Good luck," I say, averting my eyes from hers.

We were supposed to go to Lucienne's wedding the following Saturday, and she had thick and magnificent braids on her head.

"Jessie, they'll never be able to do anything, knowing that God can see them."

I hug her to me without replying.

On the way back everything is alright.

The weather is mild in Kigali. The streets are deserted and suddenly look wider. I realize that without noticing—and probably like every one of us—I had certain reference points in the city. A little shop at the street corner. Motorcycle repairers in the vicinity of a Petrorwanda gas station. Little things like that. Since the news of the assassination of the president broke, all these tableaux have disappeared from the scene. The occasional people who dare leave their houses are foreigners, or, of course, Hutus. Or those whose IDs say they are. That's my case. The others are all hiding wherever they can.

In the city there's an excitement that's both joyful and solemn. Groups of Interahamwe militia in white outfits covered with banana leaves walk around singing. Standing in their tanks, the military and the police are keeping an eye on everything. Everyone has a transistor radio glued to his ear. The radio says: "My friends, they have dared to kill our good president Habyarimana, the hour of truth is at hand!" Then there're some music and games. The host of the program, in brilliant form, quizzes his listeners: "How do you recognize an Inyenzi?" The listeners call in. Some of the answers are really funny, so we have a good laugh. Everyone gives a description. The host becomes serious again, almost severe: "Have fun, my friends, but don't forget the work that's waiting for you!"

At Camp Kigali ten Belgian UN soldiers have been killed. Belgium is pulling out. They don't want to know anything else. Even their civilians are feeling threatened and they try to pass for French at the barricades. Somewhere in Paris some sinister civil servants are rubbing their hands together: the situation is under control in Kigali, the RPF won't get in. Their straw men got the army generals and commanders together. They uttered the terrible words: *Muhere iruhande.* Literally, "Begin with one side." Neighborhood by neighborhood. House by house. Don't spread your forces out in disorderly killings. All of them must die. Lists had been drawn up. The prime minister, Agathe Uwilingiyimana, and hundreds of other moderate Hutu politicians have already fallen to the bullets of the presidential guard. To tell what they did to Agathe Uwilingiyimana is beyond me. A woman's body profaned. After the so-called *Ibyitso,* the collaborators, it'll be the Tutsis' turn. What they're guilty of is just being themselves: they're barred from innocence for all eternity.

If only by the way people are walking, you can see that tension is mounting by the minute. I can feel it almost physically. Everyone is running or at least hurrying about. I meet more and more passersby who seem to be walking around in circles. There seems to be another light in their eyes. I think of the fathers who have to face the anguished eyes of their children and who can't tell them anything. For them, the country has become an immense trap in the space of just a few hours. Death is on the prowl. They can't even dream of defending themselves. Everything has been meticulously prepared for a long time: the administration, the army, and the Interahamwe are going to combine forces to kill, if possible, every last one of them.

I've chosen to be here. The resistance leaders at Mulindi placed their trust in me and I accepted. They explained to us that the Arusha peace treaty could produce either the best or the worst of results and that the RPF needed people in all the big cities and towns.

On the eve of our departure I thought a lot about my father. In my brothers and sisters' opinion I was his favorite. Even he didn't attempt to hide it. When we were in Bujumbura sometimes he would say, "Of all my children, Jessica is the one who is most like me." A funny character, Jonas Sibomana. He would show us his torso, furrowed with scars, and would promise to leave all his goods to the one of us who could reproduce the same scars on his own body. My brother Georges, who didn't take anything seriously, answered him, "You're so broke, old Jonas, that it's not even worth it to try." Then both of them would pretend to fight and we had so much fun watching them run all over the house. My father had been a member of Pierre Mulele's resistance movement in Kwilu. Oh, he wasn't one of the important people in the group. He was just one of those peasants they give weapons to, explaining to them quickly who the enemies are. They could lose their lives in all that, but they wouldn't make a name for themselves. Jonas told us that he saw Che Guevara when the Cuban came to organize the resistance in the Congo. He also knew Kabila, and didn't have a good word to say about him. When he felt very ill, in Bujumbura, he called for me: "Go to the house where we used to live in the neighborhood of Buyenzi, and tell the owner that it's your father, Jonas Sibomana, who sent you. He'll understand." The owner and I found a big package in a hole next to a spigot. I opened it. It contained three old guns, already half rusted. When I went back to see him we had a good laugh at his joke.

I suppose that's what made me decide to interrupt my studies when I was eighteen to join the guerrillas in Mulindi.

I remember everything as if it were yesterday. There were fifteen of us young people making the road trip by night from Bujumbura to the Mushiha refugee camp. Departure the next day already, at dusk—because we always had to move about in the dark—for Mwanza in Tanzania where we had to wait for the boat—the *Victoria*—for a week. After that, it was Bukoba. There we were supposed to locate a red truck parked at the port. The leader of our group, Patrick Kagera—he was to fall later in the front line of our October 1990 offensive—started looking all around him, his nose in the air. A large man in a hat, with a scarf around his neck, passed close to him and said very quickly without stopping, "Is it you?" Later on it was in Mutukura and Kampala where we stopped seeing each other. I was staying with a family in the Natete neighborhood. In the evening, when I took a stroll in the street to stretch my legs a bit, I was puzzled to see cars driving on the left-hand side of the road. It's strange, but that's my strongest memory of Natete, cars driving on the wrong side. All I had to do was to wait for the signal for my departure. I had understood that I was not to ask any questions of my hosts.

If I were recounting all this today, one might think that I was bragging. That's not the case. Ever since 1959, every young Rwandan, at one moment or another in his life, has to answer the same question: Should we just sit back and wait for the killers, or try to do something so that our country can go back to being normal? Between our fu-

tures and ourselves, unknown people had planted a sort
of giant machete. Try as you might, you couldn't ignore
it. The tragedy would always end up catching you. Because people came to your house one night and massacred
all your family. Because in the country where you live in
exile, you always end up feeling in the way. Besides, what
could I, Jessica Kamanzi, possibly brag about? Others
have given their lives for the success of our struggle. I
have never held a gun nor participated in the military actions of the guerrillas. I stayed almost the whole time at
Mulindi to take care of the cultural activities of the resistance. Sure, I was at Arusha during the negotiations. I
typed or photocopied documents and sometimes I was
called on to give summaries to our delegates. But those
were only humble tasks. It's true that my presence in
Kigali today is not without danger. It's maybe the first
time that I've risked my life. In this country, where all the
citizens are watched night and day, my false ID card probably won't protect me for very long. I have to move all the
time. But sooner or later there'll be someone who'll ask
me some very precise questions that I'll have a hard time
answering.

While I'm walking I think back on our night watches.
We used to sing, "If three fall in combat, the two who are
left will free Rwanda." Very simple words. We didn't have
the time for poetic tricks. These words come back to me
like an echo and give me strength. The moment of liberation is at hand. Since this morning our units have been
moving on Kigali. But will they arrive everywhere in
time? Unfortunately, no. In certain places, the butchery
has already started.

Near Kyovu I see hundreds of corpses a few yards from
the barricade. While his colleagues are slitting the throats
of their victims or hacking them to bits with machetes

close to the barricade, an Interahamwe militiaman is check-ing ID cards. The visor of his helmet is turned backwards, a cigarette dangles from his mouth, and he is sweating profusely. He asks to see my papers. As I take them out of my bag he doesn't take his eyes off me. The slightest sign of panic, and I'm done for. I manage to keep my compo-sure. All around me there are screams coming from every-where. In these first hours of massacre the Interahamwe surprise me with their assiduity and even a certain disci-pline. They are really set on giving the best of themselves, if it is possible to speak this way of the bloody brutes. A woman they've wounded but are waiting to finish off a bit later comes toward me, the right part of her jaw and chest covered with blood. She swears that she's not a Tutsi and begs me to explain it to the man in charge of the bar-rier. I move away from her very quickly. She insists. I tell her dryly to leave me alone. Seeing this, the Interahamwe militiaman is convinced that I'm on his side. He blurts out in a joyful peal of laughter:

"Ah! You're hardhearted my sister, so you are! Come on, you should take pity on her!"

Then he brutally pushes the woman back toward the throat slitters before checking the ID cards again.

PART TWO | *The Return*

of Cornelius

Abidjan. Kinshasa. Nairobi. Dar es-Salaam. Addis-Abeba. Entebbe . . . Cornelius Uvimana made a mental count of the numerous landings the plane had made before arriving in Kigali. Ethiopian Airlines flight 930 on this sixth day of July, 1998, had stopped all over the place. With each new wave of passengers the stewardesses had served sandwiches and orange juice. Cornelius's stomach was turning from it. Thirty-six hours of travel. He felt worn out and dirty. Luckily, he had been able to take advantage of the stopover in Abidjan—almost an entire day—to explore the city. From his solitary lunch at the Hippopotamus Restaurant, in the Plateau district, he had, curiously, retained only a single image, and that was of the glances he had exchanged with an unknown woman. A beautiful metisse woman sitting at the bar. Her thighs were powerfully molded into a pair of faded jeans and he had seen her turn several times in his direction. Then the young woman had suddenly taken off down the stairs, disappearing forever into the crowd. That was all. Just a moment of erotic reverie stolen by chance in a foreign city and a story that would never take place. That was life. Strangers who cross each other's paths, look at each other, and are lost forever.

At the Kigali airport there was hardly anyone left in the plane. His childhood friends, Jessica Kamanzi and Stanley Ntaramira, had come to meet him. He took each of them in his arms for a long time and felt Jessica's bony body against his. She was very thin and seemed to be in bad health under her determined forehead and her deep and slightly sad eyes. While they were crossing the city in a taxi Cornelius caught Stanley Ntaramira staring at him. No doubt he was curious to see what kind of person Cornelius had become after such long years of exile. Jessica, sitting next to the driver, was, as usual, more direct:

"So who is this person who's come back home to us?"

Cornelius thought it an unusual but definitely an interesting way to put the problem. He didn't have an answer yet. All his family had perished in the genocide, except his uncle, Siméon Habineza. It was clear that everything he had experienced abroad, away from Rwanda, would only find its true meaning in what had happened four years earlier. In a certain way, his life was just beginning.

"I don't know," he replied. "Here you are welcoming me already with your trick questions!"

"And over there?" Stanley asked very quickly in order to change the subject.

It was easier to talk to them about Djibouti.

In his mind's eye Cornelius saw images of Lake Assal

and the pink cupola, of an almost perfect roundness, of Devil's Island. He thought of his excursions with Zakya. Djibouti had fascinated him. He explained to Stanley and Jessica that it was an immense expanse of stone, a country of vivid colors, often red or black. He told them that Djibouti had made him experience a strange emptiness and that no country in the world offered itself up so immodestly to the curiosity of strangers. There, everything was visible to the naked eye, including misery, which elsewhere took so much trouble to escape attention. He could not, however, speak to them about the Red Sea. He would tell them later that it had always made him think of some underwater giant, too slow and a little stupid. Cornelius had a lot of reasons to like Djibouti, beginning with his love for Zakya. But the strongest reason was perhaps this: it was the only place in the world where he had had the feeling that one could start something anew. He could have added that in Djibouti he had never felt death at his heels the way he had in his childhood in Murambi.

"So, are people there happy or not?" asked Jessica.

"They're very poor. We'll talk about it again, it's not simple. In the meantime, explain Kigali to me."

Stanley started to play the guide. They had just passed the neighborhood of Kanombé. Cornelius wanted to be shown the place where Habyarimana's plane had fallen in April 1994, but then thought better of it. He consumed the city with his gaze, trying to fathom intuitively the secret relationship between the trees standing still on the side of the road and the barbarous scenes that had stupefied the entire world during the genocide.

As for the driver, he was playing a rather strange little game: each time he thought that Cornelius was busy looking somewhere else, he studied him in his rearview mirror, as if he were trying to read something in his face. "Don't I look like a Rwandan anymore?" thought Cornelius, amused.

At Nyamirambo where Stanley lived, Cornelius took out his two suitcases and his little red sports bag.

"Well, here's someone who's coming back to us from a lifetime of exile with almost nothing," said Jessica, laughing.

Cornelius had no time to respond. The driver, who seemed to have been waiting for this moment, came up to him and asked him if he would mind writing the name of the country he had come from on a little piece of paper.

"Hmm! And why do you want that?" he asked, puzzled.

The driver explained that he collected the names of faraway countries where his customers came from.

The three friends burst out laughing.

"Did you hear that, Stan?"

"Yes," said Stan merrily, "they've been coming to us from all over the place as of two or three years ago."

"Is Djibouti far?" asked the taxi driver, who had more ideas in mind.

"Yes . . . and no," said Cornelius with a vague gesture.

So as to make up for the driver's disappointment Jessica told him that Cornelius was most probably the only Rwandan ever to have lived in that country.

Cornelius had brought some gifts for his friends. Jessica disappeared into the bedroom and came out again in a blue gandoura, gesticulating, as an excuse for dancing, to the sound of an imaginary Arabic music.

"Now for the serious things," she said. "I skipped a meeting with my committee just to see what dear old Cornelius would be like. That's done. We'll see each other later."

Stanley said that he had something to do as well, but Cornelius realized that he mainly wanted to let him rest.

"When are you going to Murambi?" asked Jessica just as she was leaving with Stanley.

"I haven't decided yet. As soon as possible, in theory."

"We could make the trip together, if it's on a weekend," suggested Stanley.

Cornelius hesitated. Without knowing why, the idea didn't appeal much to him. He wanted to be alone when he went back to the house where he had been born.

"We'll talk about it," he said.

His friends noticed his embarrassment. There was a moment of silence. Jessica succeeded in easing the atmosphere again:

"In any case, don't forget to tell Siméon that I'm still just as madly in love with him!"

Stanley came to life at the mention of Siméon's name.

"Ah! Siméon Habineza! That old man, he has such class! He's what I call a man!"

The three of them looked at each other. Up to that moment they had succeeded in keeping their memory at bay. At the mention of Siméon's name, each one of them guessed what the others were feeling and the precise day of their childhood that they were thinking of. Out of their past had just resurfaced the secret bond that united them and that was stronger than everything else. Life had separated them, but Siméon Habineza had kept them bound to each other across the years.

Alone in his bedroom, Cornelius remembered that Monday in February 1973 when, still children, the three of them had had to flee to Burundi. Twenty-five years ago already . . . It was right before the fall of President Grégoire Kayibanda. That morning two men had come to their class, holding some lists. The teacher had read out some names in a loud voice and sent some students home. Not one of those young Tutsis knew yet that he would no longer have the right to return to school. Seeing Jessica and Stan leave with the excluded group, Cornelius had thought there was a mistake. Why his friends and not him? In spite of his shyness he stood up: "Sir, you've forgotten me." The two men looked searchingly at the teacher in a severe manner. The teacher had then explained to them, laughing, "Cornelius is Dr. Joseph Karekezi's son. His father is Hutu. . . . " One of the men cut him off. "Hmm! That troublemaker Joseph Karekezi! A very bad Hutu! Hmm! He . . . he's already corrupted his son."

That same night men armed with machetes and sticks attacked the house where he had been born. Jessica and Stanley had come there to hide. Siméon had then beckoned them into the thickness of the banana grove and signaled to them not to move. Flames and screams of terror were also rising from the house next door. For two hours, lying on the ground, they had watched the attackers knock down walls, pull out posts, smash doors and windows, and set fire to anything they damned well felt like. Their faces were lit up now and then by the flames. They said that all the Tutsis had to leave the country. One of the arsonists had almost made the three kids laugh. The short-legged character was so obese that he looked like a monstrous block of fat. He had monumental buttocks and his badly buttoned red shirt revealed a round flabby stomach that hung down onto his thighs. He handled his machete, which was too long for him, with a comic clumsiness. He stopped every two minutes, out of breath, his tongue hanging out, his eyes rolled upwards, leaning on the machete planted in the ground. He had ended up sitting on the ground, his hands on his sides. While he breathed noisily as if in agony, the flames danced against his face that was twisted with pain. He looked on enviously as his sturdier companions sowed devastation around them. What was that fellow doing there? It was completely insane.

Later, in Bujumbura, the three teenagers got in the habit of hilariously imitating the gestures of the character who wanted so badly to kill people, but was too fat to manage.

That night, the killers were content to frighten people: no one had been killed during the attack. However Cornelius and his two friends witnessed a scene that would remain etched in their minds forever. Before leaving, the armed men had doused Siméon's six cows with gasoline and thrown flaming brands into the pen. Then, from the shelter of their truck, they had watched the beasts turn around and around on themselves like big balls of fire, flinging themselves at anything they saw move with a strange bellowing, then dropping, moving their legs more and more feebly, and dying in a long death rattle.

As soon as calm was restored, Siméon said to them:

"Come with me, my children. We're going to walk for a long time. I will tell your parents when I come back."

He had led them to Burundi through swampy paths along the Nyabarongo River. Many of their playmates would join them there later, because the massacres were continuing in Rwanda. Ten dead. Thousands dead. Repeated assassinations of political opponents. The tragic routine of terror.

In thinking about it again Cornelius wondered if he would be able to evoke that episode from the past with his uncle, in Murambi. Nothing was less sure. Cornelius still felt intimidated by Siméon. He still had an image of him as a sober and reserved being, with a great inner strength.

He scraped a match and held its flame to his watch. Almost one in the morning. He stood up and headed for his bed. Not being sleepy, he started his letter to Zakya. He liked to write lying down, leaning first on one elbow, then on the other. But after a few lines he realized that his ideas were no longer clear and he turned off the night light. In a few days things would maybe be better.

He fell asleep without even taking the time to unpack.

The next morning he made himself a coffee on the little gas stove. It was seven o'clock and Stanley Ntaramira, who had no doubt come home very late at night, was still sleeping. Cornelius began to sort out and classify his papers: documents and books on the history of Rwanda. He had read a lot about it during the last few years, not so much to find out about the distant past of his country as to understand the genocide. He had the impression that everything led him back to the killings of 1994. Even the scholarly speculations on Rwanda's geologic layers led him there, via secret and tortuous paths. It was as if the genocide irradiated everything with its gloomy light, sucked toward itself the most ancient and insignificant facts to give them a tragic dimension, a different meaning from what they would have had elsewhere.

A photo of Zakya slid out of an Ethiopian Airlines magazine. In seeing the slightly mocking face of his girlfriend again, Cornelius considered that his life had been a long series of ruptures but that Zakya was one of the fixed points in it. He had very quickly been struck by her look of a liberated young woman with a lively and open spirit. The material that she sometimes draped around her body, far from obscuring her figure, on the contrary highlighted her suppleness and hinted at her sensuality. Very tall—she stood taller than Cornelius, who was rather stocky, by a good head—Zakya had the slightly fragile slenderness of the people of her country.

Before his departure Cornelius had insisted on going one last time to Tadjoura. They had talked about their plans. Zakya would come as soon as he had found her a position in a high school. Maybe they needed math teachers in Rwanda, after all.

It was fate that had taken him to Zakya's country. Everything had been decided within a few weeks. In leaving Bujumbura, he didn't really know what he was doing. Later, he wondered whether he hadn't simply wanted to go somewhere where he was almost sure that he wouldn't find any of his fellow countrymen. Was he so ashamed of them? No, he didn't think so. Basically, it all boiled down to one thing: ever since his childhood, Rwanda frightened him. Admittedly, he had known mornings of pure bedazzlement there, like that day when Siméon had talked to him, on the shores of Lake Mohazi, about the birth of Rwanda. He often thought again of the child with the flute who had passed close to them then. But he couldn't forget the days of terror in his younger years when killers constantly lurked around him.

The moment when, in the banana grove, he held his breath in the company of Jessica and Stanley, left a black spot in his memory. No doubt that was why he loved the wide open spaces of Djibouti. If the killers were to come back, he could escape from them by running straight in front of him. In Djibouti, that vast and luminous land, he would never feel pinned against the wall of the houses of neighbors they were also killing.

In disparate fragments, scenes of the past and the present crossed each other in his mind. He sensed how difficult it was going to be for him to put some order into his life and he didn't like the idea. To come back to one's country—to be happy there or to suffer—was a rebirth, but he didn't want to become someone without a past. He was the sum of everything he had experienced. His faults. His cowardliness. His hopes. He wanted to know, down to the very last detail, how his family had been massacred. In Murambi, Siméon Habineza would tell him everything. He had to.

In his pyjamas, without stopping, Stanley crossed the hallway with a towel around his neck. A few seconds later, Cornelius heard him taking a shower.

When they met up again in the living room, Cornelius wanted to have some news of their childhood friends. Just as he had expected, almost all of them had been killed.

As he poured himself some coffee Stanley said to him:

"You know, you won't find many people willing to talk about those events."

"That's understandable," replied Cornelius.

He waited to see what Stanley was trying to get at.

"Jessica insists that we all go together to Murambi," he continued.

Stanley had tried very hard to sound natural, but his voice had betrayed him. Why did his friends insist so much on accompanying him to Murambi? He suddenly realized that since they had first seen each other again at the airport, Stanley had seemed concerned about him and perhaps even a bit distant from him. Did they look down on him because he hadn't done anything for the liberation of his country? They had fought. Jessica had been one of the liaison agents with the guerrillas in Kigali during the genocide. It was a dangerous mission. She could have been discovered and killed at any moment. Stanley had traveled all over the world to raise funds and explain the

RPF's struggle to foreigners. And all this time, he had been leading a peaceful existence as a history teacher in Djibouti. . . . No, his friends wouldn't hold it against him. Not them. Suddenly a terrible idea began to take root in his mind.

"Stan. Don't hide anything from me. If Siméon Habineza is dead, you've got to tell me."

At first Stanley was dumbstruck. He had the combination of composure and casualness of what many people think makes a decent fellow. But this time, Cornelius saw that he was distressed.

"Don't speak of misfortune, Cornelius."

He seemed to be holding it against him that he had thought of such an appalling thing.

"I need to know everything," said Cornelius, a bit confused. "Siméon is the sole survivor of my family."

Stanley then said in a cheerful way, adding milk to his coffee:

"Well, the only thing to know is that Siméon Habineza will never die!"

They relaxed a bit.

"We're having lunch at the Café des Grands Lacs, right near here," declared Stanley. "But beforehand, if you're not too tired, we can take a look around town."

"You're not going to work?"

Stanley was the director of one of the departments of the National Bank.

"I've taken two days off, I'll make it up one of these days. It's enough to drive you crazy: lining up numbers the whole damned day!"

Cornelius remembered that in high school in Bujumbura, Stanley, who had a gift for languages, was also known as a little genius in mathematics.

"Do you remember what you used to do with the radio when we were little, Stan?" asked Cornelius, mischievously.

"No. What are you talking about?"

"You used to say to us, Jessica and me: 'Shhh! Don't make any noise. The people who live in there and do the singing are taking a nap!' In the evening you'd put a thick blanket over it so that they wouldn't be cold. You'd really forgotten that?"

"Of course not," said Stanley, smiling. "I also climbed up on chairs to blow out the electric light bulbs. I thought they were like candles. But you never knew anything about that. I could have become a great scientist after all; that's what usually happens to children who aren't all that bright."

"Yes. You wanted to know everything, but you haven't done too badly you know, old Stan."

In their good spirits Cornelius rediscovered their former closeness. He felt a flash of happiness for the first time since his arrival the day before at being back in his own country.

While they were taking a walk Cornelius asked Stanley what his many trips on behalf of the guerrillas had taught him. Stanley answered on the spot, as if he had often thought about it.

"Almost everything about myself. I talked about our country to lots of people, in little rooms, in Bobo-Dioulasso, in Stockholm, or Denver. Nice people too, they wanted to help, but first they wanted to understand."

"Were you able to explain it to them? Sometimes it's enough to drive you mad. . . . "

"I tried, and they would say, 'Is it really just as simple as that?' That was the classic question. And when I answered 'Yes,' they would fire: 'Then why so much cruelty?' I would say, 'I don't know,' and they would find my explanation suspect. I didn't want to lie to them. But even I still don't understand all that bloodshed, Cornelius."

"The killers' real victory is the way they've succeeded in tangling everything up. People always have the impression that you're hiding something from them."

"Do you remember that long letter that I wrote you from the States?"

"Oh yes, from Florida . . . "

Cornelius remembered it perfectly. In it, Stanley talked about a meeting he had had with some students and teachers in Tampa. That day things had gone well. He had evoked the Holocaust. Would they say that the Holocaust was just a simple case of ethnic killing between Semites and Aryans? No, of course not. To say such a thing would be an insult to the memory of the victims. What it really was, was the murderous folly of the Nazis carried out against defenseless men and women. He had told them: "By the end of this one-hour talk, in Rwanda six-hundred old people and children will have been atrociously killed." And what was their crime? They were simply accused of being Tutsis. Stan wrote in his letter: "I told them: 'It has taken a very long time to render the Jewish genocide its true meaning, but nowadays it's not necessary to wait so long. What would you have done at that time if you had been able to prevent the Final Solution by simply putting some pressure on your government?"

Reading his letter, Cornelius remembered having been struck by Stanley's lucidity, dictated, no doubt, by the feeling of urgency. His goal could be summed up in a few words: let's save human lives first and talk about it later if you want.

"It was a strange letter," mused Cornelius.

"I couldn't go on. It was in May 1994, the hardest month

of the genocide. I couldn't get hold of Jessica in Kigali. So I wrote you. What that whole period of my life taught me is what makes us different from other people: no-one is born a Rwandan. You learn to become one. I read that somewhere else, and it fits our situation perfectly. It's a very slow project that each one of us takes upon himself."

"Do you think it's going to get better, eventually?"

"The government is making an effort, that's true. They've eliminated the mention of ethnicity on ID cards, and lots of other things. But the real problem is the mechanics of power in Africa. You never know what tomorrow will bring."

"Do you think it could start up again?"

"That depends on each one of us. The genocide didn't begin on the sixth of April 1994, but in 1959 through little massacres that no-one paid attention to. If there are politically motivated murders today, they need to punish the culprits straightaway. Otherwise, all that blood will be visited upon us again one day or another."

The Café des Grands Lacs was deserted, except for five or six morose-looking customers. Cornelius slid one of the white chairs across the wooden floor and sat down facing the street. Franky, the waiter, came over to him:

"The usual, boss?"

He nodded and they both smiled with a knowing look. Within a few days he and Franky had almost become friends. Cornelius almost always ordered the same meal. Passion-fruit juice and fish brochettes with grilled manioc and buttered beans.

The Café des Grands Lacs, rather cramped and cordoned off by some fine rope, had the advantage of facing Nyamirambo's main avenue. For a popular neighborhood, Nyamirambo seemed rather peaceful. The speakers hanging in a corner of the bar were playing pachanga music, while some Rwandan songs rose up from a neighboring house, a tumbledown shack, a few yards down on the left. Several tank trucks parked on the low-lying part of the road blocked the view a bit, forcing passersby to make a big detour around them.

Banal scenes in a city like any other. It was astounding to Cornelius to note that the events of 1994 had left no visible traces anywhere. Where on this avenue had they set up the famous Nyamirambo barricade? Was it there, right at the entrance to the Café des Grands Lacs, where there had been corpses that dogs and vultures came to devour? Only the city herself could have answered these questions he still couldn't ask anyone. But the city refused to show her wounds. Besides, she didn't have many. The city wasn't coming out of a war, there hadn't been any shellings, aerial bombings, or gunfire on either side of some narrow lane. The Interahamwe, who wanted live meat, had left the trees alone. Along the avenues, survivors and headsmen passed each other. They glanced at each other for a moment, then continued on their way, thinking of God knows what.

Cornelius couldn't even remember seeing any injured or mentally ill people during his walks. On the contrary, the country was intact, and people were settled in to their daily lives. Amorous rendezvous. A trip to the barber's. Franky and the young employees at the Café des Grands Lacs went about their work like waiters everywhere else in the world. They took orders, disappeared behind the counter or into the kitchen, then threaded their way again among the tables with a smile on their lips. This disdain for the tragic seemed almost suspect to him. Was it out of dignity or habit of misfortune?

Cornelius felt a light tap on his shoulder. He turned around to see Stanley's mocking smile.

"Hey, come back to earth, kiddo!"

"A little trip to Djibouti in my head," he said, lying shamelessly.

"And what's her name?"

"Zakya Ina Youssouf," said Cornelius, caught in his own trap. "She's fantastic!"

Stanley introduced the one of his two companions Cornelius had never seen before.

The other was Roger Munyarugamba.

"I've brought Barthélemy with me. . . . He wanted to meet you."

They shook hands.

"Cornelius Uvimana. I've come from Djibouti."

Barthélemy and Roger knew the other customers, and after a few minutes Cornelius realized that they were used to meeting every evening in the Café des Grands Lacs that they all familiarly called the "GL."

As soon as the newcomers were settled at his table, he started to feel ill at ease. The most unpleasant moments of his stay were the ones where he had to talk to strangers. He didn't like to see all eyes converge on him. He would just as soon have listened to the others, keeping in the background himself.

"Has Stan told them that I was a teacher in Djibouti and that I'm thinking of writing a play about the genocide? That would be awful." Sometimes the idea seemed completely ludicrous to him. He didn't want people laughing at him behind his back.

Luckily, after a few glasses of Primus and whisky, the conversation quickly started going in all directions. Only

Roger—a stocky guy with a big voice—asked him, without any obvious afterthought, why he had taken such a long detour via Abidjan to get to Kigali.

Around twelve-thirty some soldiers in fatigues and red berets parked their truck outside the café. One of them, tall, almost shy, balancing his gun in his left hand, inspected the premises, and then went out again without a word. During the few minutes he was walking through, each one of them followed him silently with their eyes. But the soldier appeared to be polite enough—there was no sign of anger on his face—and no-one seemed to have been scared.

After the soldiers' departure, an incident occurred that troubled Cornelius immensely. A voice had risen up from behind their table. Someone had shouted abruptly, "My friends, howl out your pain! Oh! I want so much to hear your pain! I have drunk blood! And now, listen carefully to me!"

Cornelius thought immediately of the thin, taciturn man sitting alone with his glass of whisky. That clear and cutting voice could only be his, and the strangeness of what he had said fit such an unusual person. He had been introduced to Cornelius by the name of Gérard Nayinzira, but everyone called him Skipper or sometimes the Sailor. Hesitating visibly before the seriousness of what he was about to say, he announced his intention to finally reveal the truth, then came out with some enigmatic reproaches —toward whom? wondered Cornelius—in the middle of a heavier and heavier silence. He wanted to correct himself, but after having hesitated a bit again, he lifted his glass, made the ice cubes clink, and said with a violence that deeply impressed Cornelius:

"Me, forgive? But you must be joking! You must be joking!"

Then he addressed those present:

"Hey! Are these people or a flock of sheep? Common animals? Tell me! And me, my blood is full of blood!"

Cornelius's first reaction was to glance over in Stanley's direction.

But he—perfectly obviously to Cornelius—avoided his look.

Finally, and despite various urgings, the Skipper announced that he was going to leave, promising to speak another time, not having succeeded that night—for which he sincerely apologized, insisting that these gentlemen not hold it against him—in saying what was in his heart.

But instead of going home, the Skipper went and put his elbows on the bar from where he started pacing the room with an absent and vaguely hostile air. For a few moments Cornelius had the impression that he was staring at him with a special intensity. It was at that moment that Barthélemy, Stanley's other friend, opened his mouth for the first time. Cornelius studied him. Thin, he had very light skin, a long face, a fine nose, and flat temples. Since his arrival, Cornelius had been struck by his red and lackluster alcoholic's eyes, but he had also suspected him of being someone of extraordinary intelligence. Up to then, Barthélemy had been content to smoke one Intore after another, his bottle of Primus in front of him, concentrating all his attention on Cornelius, who had been bothered by it.

"In life," said Barthélemy, "what is essential is for each one of us to be true to himself. The rest . . . well, the rest doesn't matter."

He stubbed out his cigarette butt in the ashtray before ordering another beer. From the way he unleashed his words, one felt he was a man sure of himself who—in solitary reflection—had formed very clear opinions on all subjects. No one answered him. It was as if each one of them was afraid to break the ambiguous charm of the moment.

Reality had just been transformed, in a more or less worrisome way, into something that had already been experienced. For Cornelius, everything converged on this general malaise: the end of this evening in a city that he hardly knew, the half-light of the café, the frozen faces, the raucous and lugubrious voices of Barthélemy and the Skipper.

He went home on foot in the company of Stanley and Roger.

"What does all that mean?"

"Nothing," said Stanley quickly.

"I see you were anticipating my question, Stan. . . . "

"Of course. Don't trust appearances. We try and forget, but sometimes it comes welling up so powerfully. No-one can do anything about it. That man escaped a massacre and . . . and, there!"

"Are you alright, Stan?"

"Why?"

"I get the feeling that you don't like to talk about this business."

"No, I hate it. Know that for once and for all I want to forget."

"But why was he looking at me like that? I don't know the guy."

"If you want to know the truth, here it is: the Skipper wasn't looking at anyone and he's already forgotten all about it."

Stanley seemed both dissatisfied and sad.

"I'm out of my depths," thought Cornelius, seeing his friend's stony face.

"I'm going to have another drink, I'm not sleepy," said

Roger, who had clearly chosen not to get involved in their discussion.

Cornelius allowed himself to be tempted.

"I'll come with you."

They went a few steps. Stanley, who was already a bit away from them, called him back and said in a low voice:

"Watch out for that guy."

"I hate him," declared Cornelius forcefully.

He was riled up and furious with everybody.

"You're also a bit tight, so be careful, kiddo," said Stanley, giving him a slap on the shoulder.

He and Roger were caught by rain in the neighborhood of Kimihurura. They went into a little restaurant run by a West African. In terms of a restaurant it was more of a smoky little hut where they sold grilled beef and chicken. Every once in a while the wind blew in rain and the customers were pressed against each other among the piles of beer and Coca-Cola crates. They sat down on a long wooden bench next to some other customers and were served whisky. Cornelius wondered to himself what he was doing in this place at this time of night and why he hated Roger so much when he hardly knew him. Being completely wet from the rain worsened his already bad mood. If Roger had brought him there, surely he had something up his sleeve. What did he want to know, that bastard? A shady guy. "If Stan told me to be careful, there must be a reason. They suspect Roger of having behaved badly during the events." But Roger was recounting, for the twentieth time in a couple of days, how he had saved wounded people during the genocide.

"I cleaned their wounds with communion wine," he said proudly.

"Not surprising," said Cornelius in a sharp tone. "The power of Jesus, no?"

He was feeling more and more drunk and ready to make a scene on the slightest pretext.

"I see that you're not taking me seriously, but I assure you, there's no better disinfectant than communion wine."

One of the people next to them on the bench, who had seemed to be asleep, turned toward Roger with a dazed look. Cornelius burst out laughing.

The rain didn't stop until half past two in the morning.

Completely drunk, they wandered the wet and deserted streets of Kigali. Roger asked him what he was going to do in Murambi. "He looks as if he's insinuating that I wasn't there when people were being killed and now I've come to bother the hell out of everyone with my pain," Cornelius thought bitterly.

"I'm going to put on a play about the genocide."

"Oh yeah?" said Roger.

Cornelius then set about inventing a crazy story, stopping often to recite passages or imitate the movements of his actors.

"Yes. At the beginning of the play there's this French general who strides across the stage with an enormous cigar in his hand. Perrichon is his name. I want people to see immediately that he's a man of utter bad faith. A pudgy guy with a mustache, wearing silk pyjamas. Want me to tell you what the general's worried about? Well, here goes: he's upset, he says they might have killed his cat during the genocides."

"The genocides?"

"Yes, the general has this damned theory about recipro-
cal genocides. Everyone tries to kill everyone else, and
afterwards there's no one left to kill anyone. Are you following me?"

By way of an answer Roger grimaced.

"The perfect asshole, this general. Hypocrite beyond the
pale. 'Of course,' he says, 'of course, some people will be
scandalized: what's all this about a man who's come to
talk to us about his cat when we're all dying?' And General Perrichon understands, he says that general or not, he
has a weakness for human rights. The defense of widows
and orphans, he knows that. Yes, he understands them.
He doesn't like what's going on in this country at all, all
that blood spilled on Rwandan soil. It's so horrible. But—
and here the general raises his little finger to show that
after the noble sentiments, the moment of pure reason is
nigh—does his cat have anything to do with it? He asks
a very precise question: Is his cat Hutu or Tutsi or Twa?
No, neither one nor the other, right? Perfect. Let everyone
follow his reasoning carefully. He's not going to get all
hung up about it, he loves that animal, he proclaims it out
loud and he insists that they prove to him—by rigorous
demonstration and not by this muddled claptrap that's in
fashion—that the death of a cat can resolve the country's political problems. He has nothing against blacks, but
aren't they exaggerating a bit? They get up to their tricks
and instead of facing up to things, they say it's the whites'
fault, that it's the cats' fault, and when they start eating
each other, the good souls say, 'Yes, but you have to understand, there's famine.' He'll state it bluntly: 'Blame it
on the famine!' Right at that moment, actors hidden in the
audience start to laugh, and he cries. 'Ah! You think that's
funny! Well, we'll just have to take things as they come!'
Are you still following me, my dear Roger?"

"Very interesting," says Roger ironically, more and more perplexed.

"Then, changing his tune, General Perrichon calls out the name of Captain Régnier. He arrives and gives the military salute: the case is entrusted to him. The captain asks, 'Excuse me, General, you did say your cat?' The captain thinks, all the same, that that's going a bit too far. Yes, says the general who lets it be understood that the animal is carrying military secrets of the utmost importance. A spy-cat, right. Things that the Anglish and the Amerloques could use to tarnish France's honor. In short, it's a state affair. 'Have we got, uh, any clues?' asks Captain Régnier. 'Our gardener disappeared three days ago,' declares the general. 'You know, that young man who's from Ethiopia, I think. Easy to recognize. Arrogant and sly. He had them tell us that he had been killed at one of the barricades, but I have my doubts. That's too simplistic, right? When they want to take it easy they telephone the boss to say, just like that, "Sir, it's the genocide, I'm dead!" Too simplistic! Find me that man, Captain!' The general exits. The captain calls in his two assistants, Pierre Intera and Jacques Hamwe, and tells them, 'Fellows, I need you again!' Pierre Intera and Jacques Hamwe are, so to speak, from the local recruits, and they've got a funny habit of holding their two machetes up crossed, toward the sky. The captain asks them: 'How do you recognize a real friend?' They answer by scraping their machetes together. 'He's there when things get rough.' Then he says to them: 'To work, lads!' And our three men torture, rape, and kill to find the Ethiopian gardener who has disappeared with General Perrichon's cat."

After watching Cornelius for a moment, Roger says in a low voice:

"You shouldn't drink. It's dangerous for you."

His voice was all changed. He was really scared. Cornelius realized that he should be quiet but he had no desire to be. He explained to Roger that he was hesitating between Médor and Sultan for the name of the cat. He shouted louder and louder into the calm of the night and Roger was terrorized.

"They go everywhere together."

"Who do you mean?"

Roger didn't understand anything any more.

"Captain Régnier and my two rogues, Pierre Intera and Jacques Hamwe. He he!"

"You're clueless, Cornelius. But I'm anxious to have a discussion with you tomorrow, when you're better," said Roger again.

"I have some ideas for the two rogues," pursued Cornelius with the pigheadedness of a drunk. "Throughout the play they'll keep their two machetes raised toward the sky and crossed. But I've already told you that, I think. They're hardly going to open their mouths. Their only way of talking will be to scrape their machetes against each other. I'm playing with that idea, I'm playing with it. . . . "

They arrived in front of Roger's house. Roger was visibly grateful finally to be able to get rid of Cornelius.

"So what's the end of your story going to be, are they going to find the cat or what?" he asked, ringing the doorbell of his house.

"Oh no! You don't know me very well, I'm not going to let that half-wit of a General Perrichon have his way. Oh yes, I forgot to tell you, all that time his wife hasn't stopped blubbering. She's going to leave him, because she won't have anything to do with a general who's incapable of protecting a cat from an Ethiopian gardener in times of war. He's going to go crazy with sorrow and at the end he's going to wander on to the stage going 'meow . . . meow . . . '"

"Good night. We'll talk tomorrow. I'm serious."

Cornelius continued his path alone, meowing all the way to Nyamirambo.

Cornelius got off the minibus and stood for a few minutes on the side of the road. Several sandy alleys followed a dip for about a hundred yards and then climbed back up toward the hill. He didn't know which one led to Jessica's. From her instructions he only remembered that he would see, not far from the bus stop, a row of barbershops. He went in at random among the tortuous little streets. They were all torn up by rivulets of dirty water. Next to a big open gutter lay pieces of rusted sheet metal, tin cans, cardboard packaging, and fallen branches with leaves sullied by mud. Every once in a while nauseating fumes would suddenly saturate the atmosphere and he redoubled his step. Arriving behind him and driving very slowly, an old white delivery car was stirring up lots of dust in its wake. Cornelius pinned himself against a wall and let it pass. A charcoal seller had, unfortunately, set up shop across the way, and a black cloud wafted up toward the sky. It was astounding. At the corner of an alleyway a melancholy man was selling, on a rickety table, shoes that were beyond repair and completely bent out of shape. Would someone really stop to buy such a thing? It seemed almost desperately absurd. He stopped near some dressmakers' workshops; their yellow walls were decorated with gaudily colored portraits of singers and athletes. In the past few days he had noticed the hills from afar, walking along the grand avenues of Kigali. Then, they had seemed sublimely beautiful to him. But now, the city was showing him her hidden side. Nothing, up to then, had hinted at the existence of these hovels, so gloomy, cramped, and claustrophobic. Sinking down on themselves, they looked ready to collapse at any moment. It was absolute chaos. Everything seemed out of place, zigzagging, dilapidated, twisted, makeshift, and decrepit. Never had he had such direct and violent contact with poverty. Confronted by this scene, so unexpected to him, he felt almost betrayed. What must this be like in the rainy season? Hardest for Cornelius was that he couldn't even imagine a day when things would be a bit better. Nevertheless, nothing struck him so much as the silence of this overpopulated hill. It wasn't altogether clear, but it seemed to him that he hadn't seen any happy groups of children, any neighbors calling out to each other across their fences or simply chatting at the entrance to their houses anywhere.

He had almost forgotten that he was looking for Jessica's house. After an hour of wandering he suddenly found himself back on the road that ran along the other side of the hill and he retraced his steps. A dirty, ragged child passed in front of him whistling. A little whippersnapper, bruised by poverty, one among hundreds of thousands of others. It was truly unbearable.

He listened carefully and thought he recognized one of Koffi Olomidé's tunes coming from the boy's mouth.

"Hey, kid!"

The boy stopped.

"Can you show me the street where all the barbershops are?"

"It's on the other side, papa. Come with me."

Jessica lived modestly—renting, she explained to him—a Kyovu-of-the-Poor house. Cornelius did his best to ignore the sorry state of the living room. A low table and some armchairs were set on the cement floor. The walls had just been repainted. Only a tiny window let in any air, and for the first few minutes Cornelius had trouble breathing normally. The house seemed dead. Nonetheless, some other renters occupied the right wing of the building. Cornelius only became aware of it when he saw them coming and going on the walkway on the other side and in the courtyard. However, he didn't notice any embarrassment on Jessica's part, and that put him more at ease.

"So, how are things, Tadpole?" she blurted out, laughing, as soon as he had dropped onto the couch.

Cornelius stared wide-eyed.

"What did you call me?"

"That was the nickname we gave you in Bujumbura, wasn't it?"

"Ah . . ."

He had forgotten.

"You had a really big head, so we gave you that nickname. Besides, you were quite ugly."

"That's sorted itself out, hasn't it?"

"You've really filled out since then, but you don't look too bad for an old guy of thirty-seven."

Jessica's badly buttoned shirt revealed her bony chest. Her body was dry and graceless. He thought that she must have been very ill.

I was Tadpole . . . Stan was the little whiz-kid at school. And her? wondered Cornelius. What had her childhood really been like? Memories of Jonas Sibomana, Jessica's father, came back to him. Short appearances in Bujumbura. He would leave again, but no one could ever say where. In the sixties he had belonged to some guerrilla group or another and his life had remained shrouded in mystery. He adored Jessica and wanted to shape her in his image. And then Jessica's mother. A very early retreat into silence and madness. She had hallucinations and talked to herself in the streets of their neighborhood of Buyenzi. Dead at an early age. In Djibouti, Cornelius had received a letter from Jessica. She told him: "My mother played a much bigger role in my choices than even I had ever imagined when she was alive. Her image follows me everywhere. She remains, even in her tomb, the secret witness to my life."

Cornelius pointed to an ashtray full of cigarette butts on the little table.

"You shouldn't smoke so much, Jessica. You're destroying yourself."

"I got into the habit in Arusha."

"Arusha?"

"Yes. I was with the RPF delegation. We hardly ever slept. So I tried to hold up as best I could. Cigarettes and cups of coffee. When we went to clubs there, we would speak Swahili, not Kinyarwanda, so as not to attract the attention of the Tanzanians."

Cornelius was unwinding with the passing minutes.

"I'm going to ask you something, and if you think it's stupid . . . "

"If I think it's idiotic, I'll enjoy making fun of you!"

"OK. Have you ever killed anyone?"

"Ah!" she said. "No. But when they were taking Kigali, I was with our people in Rebero. We sent the others on ahead to the top of the hill and from there I saw how they shot them, like rabbits."

A little bit before eleven o'clock a girl of about twenty arrived with a basket on her head.

"Nicole is my cousin. She's going to make lunch for us."

Cornelius stayed at Jessica's house until the end of the day. It was as if each one of them had kept secrets in reserve for the day they would see each other again. Cornelius brought up again the play he wanted to write. It was the first time he had done so so naturally.

"The play on the genocide? Roger told me about it."

"Hmm, I talked to Roger about it the other night. I think I said some stupid things. I was really out of it, I overdid it on the whisky."

"Oh, yes! He's told everyone about your evening. He says that you're an artist."

Jessica also promised him that she'd help him put on his play. Then, pointing around the living room with a weary gesture, she added:

"You see how I live . . . times are hard."

Cornelius avoided looking at her.

"Do you regret it Jessica?"

Jessica was silent for a moment and then answered:

"When things are really hard, I have to admit that I feel adrift. But then I immediately feel ashamed for having thought so. No, when all's said and done, it doesn't really matter what happens to some or to others, or even to the country. We fought to make Rwanda normal. That's all. It was a good fight."

"But you're still doing important things."

Jessica had got involved as a volunteer in numerous organizations that help orphans of the genocide and rape victims.

"If some day they have the means to give me a little salary, so much the better. In the meantime, there are all these wounds to bandage."

Cornelius sensed that Jessica wasn't used to opening herself up.

"Yes, there are lots of things to be done in this country, if people hadn't been so poor, we wouldn't have come to that," he said.

"Cornelius, everyone knows that. But we live in such a bizarre period. In Africa, in Europe, everywhere, the few people who still want to change the world are almost ashamed to say so, they're afraid of being taken for idiots."

Jessica was no doubt thinking wistfully of her father's times. In spite of their mediocre results, those revolutionaries had at least tried to get things moving.

She told him that sometimes she tried to understand and to accept the horror.

"I need to believe that we can live with it. It puts my mind at ease."

"Yes," said Cornelius, "we've never seen so many appalling things all at the same time. The Balkans. Algeria. Afghanistan. And did you know that in Sierra Leone they just mutilate their victims? That's worse than anything else. I don't know where they find the strength to cut off the arms and legs of a little girl before letting her go. And no one gives a damn."

"No, Cornelius, not many people really give a damn. I thought the way you do in 1994. I was mad with rage seeing all those heaps of dead bodies in Kigali. But you know all too well, after the genocide, life continued. They massacre people somewhere else, and we feel helpless. That's what's terrible: we can't do anything. It would take an entire lifetime. Our days are so short and the killers have so much more energy than decent people! Moreover, they're happy just killing the people around them, they don't even need to know that the rest of the world exists. It's easy for them to win the game."

During lunch they spoke longer about Zakya than the first time.

"She's going to come here and live with me, but first I have to find two openings in a school."

"Ah! I didn't see you living on your playwriting."

"I'm not mad."

"What's she like, Zakya Ina Youssouf?"

"She's got character. You'll see, you two'll get along well."

Zakya. Her affectionate scolding. He was beginning to miss her. Their farewells at the Djibouti airport. He could read the anxiety on her face as she waved one last time. What would become of him far away from her? Zakya must surely have been asking herself that question. She imagined Rwanda as a country completely devastated by murderous combat that could flare up again at any moment. In any case, she had always had the impression that Cornelius would be in danger anywhere. This worry of protecting Cornelius from himself made of her a woman too mature for her twenty-eight years. Cornelius sometimes even thought of her more as a big brother to him than a girlfriend. She had almost made him promise that he would write to her as soon as he got to Kigali. He promised himself that in his letter he would tell her about all the little things that he was experiencing. Why would he speak to her only about death?

"From the first few days of our meeting, she wanted to know everything about Rwanda," he said to Jessica.

"Well, of course, she had the same old stereotypes in her head: two ethnic groups who've hated each other since time immemorial."

"Of course. I tried to explain it to her patiently. I told her that it wasn't true and especially that the first massacres dated from 1959 and not from the beginning of time."

That had been a difficult period for Cornelius in his relationship with Zakya. In spite of a gnawing irritation he forced himself to remain calm. He and Zakya were still only good friends, but he was set on disabusing her of certain prejudices.

However, Zakya was not easy to convince. One day when he found her a little less reticent, he explained to her that there had never been any ethnic groups in Rwanda and that nothing distinguished the Twa, the Hutu, and the Tutsi. Straightaway a flash ran across Zakya's face. Worried that that meant she might be taking him for a liar, he threw himself into some rather chaotic explanations. "We have the same language, the same God, Imana, the same beliefs. Nothing divides us."—"Yes, it does," replied Zakya spitefully: "between you there's this river of blood. After all, that's not nothing. Stop making things up." Then she added, "I'm not an idiot, and you've got to tackle the problems of your country in some other way if you want to solve them." He was scared. Besides, could he tell her in all good faith that things were as simple as that? What meaning could one give to the violence of his country? Maybe it was absurd of the victims to keep proclaiming their innocence so obstinately. And what if this radical punishment—the genocide—was a response to some very ancient crime that no-one wanted to hear about any more? "Now that I'm in Rwanda, I'm going to ask Siméon Habineza all these questions," he thought. He wasn't afraid of the truth, he had also come back to learn it.

He admitted to Jessica:

"Zakya caused me to doubt. I went back to studying the history of Rwanda. But I didn't find any answers there. The documents prove that the Hutu and the Twa were oppressed long ago by the Tutsi. I am Hutu but I do not want to live with that legacy. I refuse to ask of the past more meaning than it can give to the present. Take the example of the Afrikaaners in South Africa. They were real foreigners, those ones, and they turned out to be infinitely more cruel to the blacks of that country than anywhere else. But it ended up getting settled over there. Why not here? When Mandela won, the Soweto blacks didn't say 'We're going to kill them all, down to the very last one!'"

Jessica smiled.

"I completely agree with you, no one would have accepted that, no one would have said 'Oh, those poor South African blacks, you've got to understand them, they suffered so much from the arrogance of white racists for three centuries!'"

"But that's the kind of thing they're saying about Rwanda today," remarked Cornelius.

"Yes," answered Jessica, "and that should make us think. Respect is earned."

It was on that day—in Obock, north of Djibouti—that an idea was born in his mind that would not leave him during the course of his years in exile. He had thought, as he was looking at Zakya angrily, "After all, Rwanda is an imaginary country. If it's so difficult to talk about in a rational way, maybe it's because it doesn't really exist. Everyone has his own Rwanda in his head and it has nothing to do with the Rwanda of others."

"Did she end up understanding, Zakya?"

"Yes. She was especially moved by my feeling of helplessness. It's true that we lived the genocide together. She's the one from whom I learned of Habyarimana's death."

One morning, Zakya had leaned toward him in the staff room: "You're so busy grading exams. I'm sure you didn't listen to the radio last night. . . . "

His heart started beating fast. It had started up again, of course. It always started up again.

They went out and she told him that President Juvénal Habyarimana's Falcon 50 had been shot down in flight the day before. Cyprien Ntaryamira, the Burundian head of state, had also been in the plane. There were no survivors, and accusations were flying everywhere: the Belgians, the French, the RPF, and the Hutu Power extremists.

Cornelius had called his father. At the other end of the line Doctor Joseph Karekezi was tense, but calm. "Of course," he declared with a rather reassuring serenity, "the hoodlums and fanatics will take advantage of the situation to attack innocent people." But he was entirely optimistic. "Everything will settle down quickly." Overcoming a certain reserve, he questioned his father: "Won't they attack you because of the stance you've taken in the past?" Doctor Karekezi had told him not to worry. Cornelius had, however, perceived a slight annoyance in his voice. "The fact that I'm so removed from Rwanda is probably making me think that the situation is more serious than it really is. Maybe that's what's irritating my father," he thought, almost relieved. Next, he discussed things with his mother, Nathalie, and joked a bit with Julienne and François. Everything seemed more or less normal.

But Doctor Karekezi had guessed wrong: every day the news was more dramatic. When he was unsuccessful at getting his father or any other member of his family on the phone, he simply said to Zakya, "I know what that means." Around them, nobody seemed to know that there was something going on in Rwanda. Their solitude during this trial brought them closer to each other.

After having listened to him with the utmost attention, Jessica said kindly:

"You're going to be able to build something, you and Zakya. That's good in any case."

"On that count, there's nothing to fear. We're made to get along."

Jessica told him the story of her friend Lucienne.

"She was going out with a guy named Valence Ndimbati. I've never seen two young people so in love with each other. Besides, everyone knew it. You'd see them everywhere, and they were due to get married in April 1994. Then there were the killings. At first, he protected her, but one day he rushed at her with a machete, shouting, 'No love today!' Lucienne was obsessed by that scene, she couldn't believe it, she talked about it all the time, laughing and crying at the same time. She ended up killing herself three months ago."

"And you, Jessica, how's your love life?"

He didn't imagine that it could be very simple. She was a woman with character, the kind that scares men. Her response surprised him.

"It's been a lot richer than you might have thought. Don't be shocked if I tell you this, but I like feeling a man move inside my body. It does me good."

Sex wasn't the kind of topic that made Cornelius feel at ease.

"I'm talking about a real relationship of love."

"Ah!" Jessica burst out laughing, "What a little angel!"

"OK, let's say . . . "

"You're making fun of me."

"I have my little theories about it, you know: we only love once in a lifetime. The question is to know which person it is."

"That depends. Zakya is the only one to have counted in mine."

"You're lucky, both of you. For me, there's one person

whose image often comes back to me, I can't manage to forget him, but I really don't know if that man is the love of my life."

In spite of her ironic tone, she seemed very bitter. Cornelius was filled with a sudden sadness. He found it unfair that after having given so much Jessica could not be happy, just because she wasn't beautiful. One man had, undoubtedly, understood Jessica, but destiny had placed itself across their path. Another painful secret, the blood extracted from her by the genocide.

"He was killed . . . ?"

Jessica let out a joyful peal of laughter.

"Not at all! What's got into you, Cornelius, that you think that no one in this country is still alive?"

They set off for Ntarama. Jessica was a good driver. The track was so bumpy that the trip lasted almost two hours. The dust stirred up by the Datsun dyed the dwarf bananas closest to the road red. Cornelius's gaze was lost in the distance, among the hills whose summits were full of softness, resembling, in the blue-tinged mist, sails pushed along slowly by the wind. Several times they passed trucks loaded with bunches of tiny green bananas and Jessica asked him if he didn't want to buy some.

"I'm crazy about them. Maybe on the way back."

"I'm not sure that you'll still feel like having them on the way back."

"Why do you say that?"

"We're going to see some terrible things, Cornelius."

On the Kanzeze Bridge Jessica said to him: "During the genocide on this river, the Nyabarongo, they counted up to forty thousand cadavers floating at the same time. You couldn't even see the water any more."

"I saw the pictures on television in Djibouti."

"And what do foreigners say when they're shown such things?"

"Nothing, Jessica. The rare few who are interested are sincerely upset. They think that Hutus kill Tutsis and Tutsis kill Hutus, that's all."

"You should have explained it to them."

It was the first time that he felt a shade of reproach in Jessica's voice.

"I tried, but very quickly you're overcome by their sympathetic smiles. You tell them: stop all your nonsense about hatred from time immemorial, it began in 1959! You tell them everything and they're happy to nod their heads somewhat skeptically."

"It's very hard, I know," said Jessica, parking under some trees.

They had arrived.

Just as they were about to go through the enormous door of the Ntarama parish church, a group of peasants sitting on the grass a few yards away on the left caught Cornelius's attention. They all turned toward Cornelius and Jessica at the same time, observing them in silence but with keen curiosity.

Inside the parish grounds Cornelius saw for the first time remains of victims of the genocide. On two long tables, inside a rectangular straw hut, human remains were exhibited: skulls on the right, and an assortment of other bones on the left. On a piece of paper caught on a little bouquet of flowers someone had written by hand, "The innocent do not die, they rest." At the far end of the parish grounds, on the left, a larger building. The caretaker was explaining things to a group of visitors there. They joined them and saw from their naïve questions and overwhelmed faces that they were foreigners. The care-taker, a small man, had a flat nose and his hair, which contrasted with the apparent youthfulness of his face, was completely white. Dressed in a very dirty blue shirt, he seemed intimidated by the visitors and stood there hum-bly, his two hands crossed at thigh height. In this second building the bodies were to be found in the same state that the killers had left them in, four years earlier. Shreds of clothing still clung to the bodies and a comb lay carelessly next to a wooden bench. The explosion of grenades had left luminous little holes in the ceiling. The caretaker was giving details in a monotone voice:

"The Interahamwe militia arrived around eleven o'clock in the morning, on an April day. The Tutsis had come to take refuge in their parish, but the priest was no longer there. I hid in the marshes, among the papyrus reeds. For several days I heard nothing but the barking of dogs."

He also said that of the one hundred and twenty thou-sand Tutsis in the town, sixty-six thousand had been killed.

Outside, the peasants, still motionless on the grass, watched them leave in silence.

From Ntarama they set off for the church of Nyamata.

Twenty-five to thirty thousand cadavers were on display in the stately red brick building. Another caretaker led them first to crypt no. 1, a yellow room located in the basement, lit by ten or so electric light bulbs. There too, remains were heaped onto a long table covered by fine sand. At one end stood a preserved body almost intact.

"Who was that young woman?" asked Cornelius, turn-ing toward the caretaker.

"Her name was Theresa. Theresa Mukandori. We all knew her very well," answered the caretaker.

The young woman had her head pushed back and the scream extracted from her by the pain had been frozen on her still grimacing face. Her magnificent tresses were disheveled, and her legs wide apart. A stake—of wood or of iron, Cornelius didn't know, he was too shocked to notice—had remained lodged in her vagina.

All that he could do was to shake his head nervously. He remembered the words of a famous African American intellectual after passing through Nyamata. Completely traumatized, he had declared on television: "I've been wrong all my life. After what I saw in Rwanda, I think that blacks are, in fact, savages. I recognize my mistake. I never want to fight for anything ever again." Cornelius had been indignant seeing the man holding forth with such cynicism. But at present, he at least understood why he had lost his head.

Cornelius turned toward Jessica, hoping absurdly for the beginning of an on-site explanation. It was as if he'd never been aware of the atrocities committed in the country. He was about to let his rage explode at Jessica.

But she, impassive, pretended not to have noticed anything. She was hearing Theresa's voice again, in front of that very church: "Jessie, they'll never be able to do anything, knowing that God can see them." The dreadful dialogue with her friend was still going on, four years down the road. She thought, with sudden violence: "In those days, Theresa, God was looking elsewhere. . . . "

"Theresa's brother is one of the Nyamata survivors," said the caretaker again. "He wanted a decent grave for his sister, but the authorities pleaded with him to leave her body as it was, so that the whole world could see it."

During the last few minutes the odor had become frankly intolerable. Cornelius stepped back toward the entrance-way to get some of the pure outside air.

Jessica joined him and they visited crypt no. 2 in the rear courtyard of the church. No sooner had he entered when Cornelius was literally propelled outside by the stench that came from within.

A second caretaker was listening to the radio on a concrete flagstone. Very different from his colleague, he had a terribly bony face and seemed to float about in his dirty shirt and his trousers patched at the knees and thighs. Cornelius was immediately struck by his lively eyes half hidden by the visor of his black cap. He spoke, a little bent forward, and his shrill voice had something unique about it.

"In Rwanda," he declared in an overly succinct style, "since 1959 one part of the population, always the same one, massacres the other, always the same one. When there were rumors of massacre in the hills, thousands of Tutsis converged on God's House. Then, two days later, the soldiers and the Interahamwe arrived with grenades, guns, and machetes."

The caretaker also showed them two tombs in the churchyard:

"The priest buried here was a very pious man. He died before the events. He had a heart attack when he learned that Pope John Paul II was coming to Rwanda. The tomb next to it is an Italian nun's. Her name was Antonia Locatelli. Two years before the genocide, when she saw that they were going to do bad things, she said on a foreign radio station: 'what they're doing to the Tutsis in Rwanda is not good, we can't just stand there with our arms crossed.' Afterwards, some men went to her house to kill her."

Jessica drove Cornelius back to Kigali in the early afternoon. The acrid odor of decomposing bodies remained like a stinking little ball, diluting slowly in his blood.

"I've got to give the car back," said Jessica.

A friend had lent it to her.

In downtown Kigali Cornelius was once again surprised to find people going about their daily business. Cars and motorcycles parked all over the place. Street kids offering all kinds of petty services. They had to make a big detour because the street in front of the American embassy had been blocked off since the anti-American attacks in Nairobi and Dar-es-Salaam, a few days earlier.

"I'll buy you a sandwich at the Glaçon and we'll walk for a bit, because you're leaving tomorrow for Murambi," said Jessica. "Is that OK with you?"

"Perfect," said Cornelius mechanically, still haunted by what he had just seen in Nyamata and Ntarama.

They took a long walk.

Once again Cornelius felt the persistence with which Kigali continued to elude him. Never knowing where he was, he was sometimes disconcerted to discover abruptly, at the end of an avenue, the entire city at his feet. Even though the air was both pure and fresh, he sometimes had a slight sensation of suffocation climbing up the hillside.

But it was on that day that for the first time a fragment of truth unveiled itself to him. There was no longer the shadow of a doubt: Jessica had something to tell him but she didn't dare do it. It must be very serious.

Night caught them in the neighborhood of Kyaciru.

Cornelius suggested that he accompany her to the Café des Grands Lacs where Stanley and his friends would be.

Instead of answering, she pulled him to her tightly, and walked along with her hand on his back. It was a gesture full of affection. He thought: "She's going to make the decision."

They were standing against a balustrade that ran along a deserted cliff. Cornelius didn't know the name of the place. The houses below them gave him the fleeting illusion of being next to the sea. Darkness rendered the hills almost invisible. At this time of day one could only guess at their faraway shapes and the city lights seemed to be suspended in emptiness. It looked as if the hills had stars at their feet.

Jessica's blue gandoura—the one he had brought her from Djibouti—flapped in the wind.

"I know you have something to tell me, Jessica."

"That's right," she uttered slowly, moving away from him. "Siméon asked us to talk to you."

He felt relieved.

Finally, to know.

"Stan and you?"

"Yes, but you'll learn to understand Stan. He did his duty during the war and he no longer wants to talk about what happened. Stan is much too normal for this country."

Jessica's mind was always restless. Cornelius suspected a lot of violence and a secret madness about her that was almost impossible to discern at first glance.

"That's not the case with you, is it?" he said. "You'll never have peace of mind."

Jessica raised her eyes toward him:

"But it's not about me. It's about your father, Doctor Joseph Karekezi. He's not dead, Cornelius. . . . "

In a flash, and with a lucidity that he could never explain, even several years later, Cornelius had a presentiment of what must have happened. He asked no question, and Jessica continued:

"Tomorrow you're going to Murambi, and you should know that your father organized the massacre of several thousand people there. The carnage at the Murambi Polytechnic, that was his doing. You should also know that he had your mother, Nathalie Kayumba, your sister Julienne, your brother François, and all his in-laws killed there."

Jessica was silent.

They both kept their eyes fixed on the emptiness.

For several seconds Cornelius didn't react.

Then something amazing happened: he smiled.

He would often have cause to think of that smile during the weeks and months to follow. It was only then that he understood why so many survivors of the genocide had recounted their suffering to him, interrupting themselves sometimes by nodding their heads and laughing incredulously.

So stupefying was Jessica's revelation, that Cornelius didn't doubt it for a single instant. But to erase the bad impression that he believed he had made on Jessica he said:

"It's hard for me to believe you. I spoke to my father several times when the massacres started. He was horrified. Is it possible that he could have done that?"

"But you know it's true," said Jessica softly.

Cornelius merely nodded his head, vanquished.

"I don't know why I smiled just then."

"Don't worry, I'm not shocked. I've seen the same thing so many times."

"My father, Jessica!"

"Yes. Your father."

"It's so bizarre. Even though he was Hutu, my father fought all his life, he tried to start a movement against impunity. He took risks."

"Afterwards, he changed. Doctor Joseph Karekezi hadn't been the same for a long time, but nobody knew it. Only he can say what happened in his head. He couldn't stand, for example, being married to a Tutsi anymore."

"He fled with the others?"

"He was evacuated during Operation Turquoise. The French were occupying the Polytechnic, on top of the mass graves of Murambi, and your father was the one who talked to them. No one ever heard anything more about him."

Cornelius's head was on fire. It was buzzing with all kinds of feelings and confused ideas. He was certain only of one thing: from that day on his life would not be the same. He was the son of a monster.

"You must have found my idea for a play out of place, Jessica."

"Not really. I simply took it as a sign of the extent to which you considered yourself innocent."

Now, his return from exile could no longer have the same meaning. From now on, the only story he had to tell was his own. The story of his family. He had suddenly discovered that he had become the perfect Rwandan: both guilty and a victim.

He asked:

"How many died in Murambi?"

"Between fifty and sixty thousand."

"Just at the Polytechnic?"

"Yes."

"Just imagine, Jessica," he said, aghast.

Scrupulous as ever, Jessica had to correct herself:

"The number of victims is controversial. Some people say forty-five thousand and others say that there were fewer. A survivors' association, Ibuka, is currently counting the dead by the skulls found at the site. We'll soon know."

"It's bizarre, people think that forty-five thousand deaths aren't very much for Africans, don't they?"

"Yes, but we've never done anything to show them that we respect human life."

They were quiet again. After a moment he said forcefully:

"It's really good that you spoke to me before I left for Murambi."

"That's how Siméon Habineza wanted it. Otherwise, maybe I wouldn't have had the courage. Cornelius, listen: after a genocide, the real problem is not the victims but the executioners. To kill almost a million people in three months took a lot of people. There were tens or hundreds of thousands of killers. Many of them were fathers. And you, you're just the son of one of them."

"Do you think that's going to console me?"

"I hope not. You have a long path to take in your heart and in your mind. You're going to suffer a lot, and that might be good for you."

"I'll be alone," he said.

"Yes, you'll be alone. Now, it's time to go home, you have to leave very early tomorrow morning."

"I'll wait for you in Murambi all the same, you and Stan."

"I'll come with Stan next month. Siméon asked us to do that, too."

That evening, Cornelius did not go to the Café des Grands Lacs.

PART THREE | *Genocide*

Aloys
Ndasingwa

At dawn we started putting up the first cordon around the
Nyamata church. The thousands of Inyenzi who were taking refuge in that House of God thought that we would
never dare attack them. Those cockroaches will find out
soon enough that you should never attribute good intentions to your enemy. According to our information, they've
even organized teams to prepare meals, to look after children, and to cut down trees for firewood and things of
that sort. But they should have been wondering why the
Nyamata priests, in seclusion for three days now, are fast-
ing and praying without stopping. The priests knew.

It's time for action.

All the same, someone must have told the refugees that
they were caught in a trap. There was a sudden movement of the crowd, then a tremendous cry rose up from
inside the church. They were shouting, "They're here!

The Interahamwe are here!" as they banged violently on the door. Some stones were thrown in our direction. We dodged them, grinning. Some of them tried to jump over the fence. They literally fell at our feet. They were the first to be eliminated. Some members of the presidential guard arrived. As soon as they entered the parish compound, the screams became more intense. They flung some grenades and shot several rounds of automatic fire into the pile. Then they signaled to us to go in. People were running in all directions. There were lots of them: twenty-five or thirty thousand? I would never have thought that the Nyamata church could hold that many people. We didn't make any exceptions. An old woman said to us, "My children, let me pray one last time." A little old lady, all wizened. It's crazy, the number of people who've asked to pray one last time since yesterday. Our commander answered the old woman with an air of false astonishment, "Ah! Mama, didn't you know? We spent the night in heaven and we fought the God of the Tutsis there until dawn! We killed him and now it's your turn." With a single stroke of his machete he sent her head to the devil.

We spent the night on the grounds. We had a good time with the women. When they're not too bad looking, we liquidate them last. After all, we're young, and you've got to live it up.

The next day, around noon, everything was finished.

The prefect arrived for a little follow-up. A guy in glasses. He was wearing an immaculate beige suit, and had put on some cologne. With his hands in his pockets he looked suspiciously at the bodies scattered throughout the parish grounds. It was clear that he was looking for something to reproach us about. I don't like that little guy, and at the slightest signal from our boss, I'll beat him up. You take one look at his hands and you know he's never held a machete. They come from the university and they order everyone around, those bastards. Why? It's not fair. If the boss tells me, "Aloys, go ahead," that guy is dead. "Are they all good and dead?" he asked, grimacing. Our commander, who was very angry now, replied that he could check. That's all the prefect was waiting for. He gave a little sidelong smile and said, "Alright, we'll see." He gestured to two of his men, ordering them to proceed with the checking. They signaled to us to move back, then threw tear gas grenades on top of the bodies piled under our eyes. The Inyenzis who were hiding underneath the bodies were already having a hard time breathing. The tear gas made them sneeze loudly and all we had to do was lay our hands on them. They opened their eyes wide when they saw us, stunned. It was really funny. No dummy after all, that prefect. We discovered four Inyenzis who were pretending to be dead. The little sneaks. The prefect said dryly, "Four is too many." Our commander protested: "And afterwards?" He has balls, our commander. A real warrior. He's not one to let people take advantage of him. The prefect said: "You can't even comprehend that tomorrow those four will be telling lies to the newpaper. You don't even understand that, do you? I really wonder how they could have trusted an idiot like you." Then things heated up. "I don't give a damn about the newspaper," yelled our commander, "and you, if you're really a man, come and join in with us!" He went toward the prefect and wiped his blood-covered machete on his lovely beige suit. Ah! Ah! The prefect was shocked by his audacity. He was about to slap the commander, but the commander caught his hand in mid-air, twisted it, and pinned it behind his back. He held him like that for a few minutes, calling the prefect a faggot. The prefect was grimacing and his glasses had fallen on the ground. You should have seen him. We had a lot of fun. Then he picked up his glasses, saying to one of his followers, "Incident at Nyamata. Four survivors. Assault against the authorities. Note the date and the time, please." Then he said very coolly, bending slightly forward, "Gentlemen, goodbye, and thank you." He walked solemnly back to his black car. One of his men opened the door for him and he sat down in the back, looking at us with displeasure, one last time.

Before we left we took anything that might be worth it: jewelry, watches, money, sunglasses, shoes, and piles of other little stuff. A belt, a disposable lighter. Socks that weren't too worn. They could still be used. We put everything together to divvy up among ourselves at the end of the day. That was a good idea our commander had; it's good for a commander to be fair, that way they respect you and there's no fighting. Among other groups of Interahamwe the fellows are already getting into fights: one of them wants to kill a girl and another wants to keep her for his nights, or vice versa. That's just human nature. I'd be happy to, but when you start to let emotions enter into the picture you just can't stop, and it's the work that suffers.

Once we were outside we saw a pack of dogs roaming around Nyamata. Gangs of children were waiting for us to leave so they could get into the church. There were so many cadavers that there was always a chance that the little ones would find something. I've even been told that they play football with the skulls, but I haven't seen that with my own eyes yet.

Marina Nkusi

We called him Tonton Antoine. For as far back as I can
remember, I always saw him at the house. He was my father's best friend. Actually his only friend, I think. Already, when I was a little girl, I had the feeling that he
wasn't like anyone else we knew. He didn't laugh very
much, but he loved doing magic tricks with cards. Pro-
jecting the shadows of his fingers against a wall, he could
also create tortoises or dragonflies. As soon as I saw him
arrive I would rush out to meet him. He would lift me
up on his shoulders and run around our place singing,
"Marina has an airplane, Tonton Antoine is little Marina's
airplane!" I was, I think, one of the few people who could
cheer him up.

A few days after the events, he came to the house a first
time. He and my father talked for a long time in low
voices.

We knew that he was in charge of several barricades in Kibuye. Nonetheless, he had a sweet face, if a little bit sad, just as I'd known him from my earliest childhood.

When he left, my father seemed to be very preoccupied.

"Does he know that we're hiding those little ones here?" asked my mother, worried.

"No, but he says I should take up my machete like all the other men."

"Ah?"

"I refused. I can't do that."

My mother said nothing. After a while he cried out again:

"Yes, I refused!"

Two days passed.

Tonton Antoine came back.

He and my father locked themselves away again in the living room. For the first time in my life I heard Tonton Antoine shout.

After this second meeting my father started to change. He talked to himself, wandering from one room to another: "Ah! I can't agree to do it, those people have never done anything to me! It's savagery!"

The next instant he would say that he had to protect us. If he didn't do anything, the Interahamwe were going to come and kill everyone in the house. The third day, not being able to stand it any more, he took up his machete. My mother and I wanted to keep him from going out. Then he screamed, "Don't you watch the television? It's like all wars, you kill people and then it's over!"

He went to the barricades. They tell us that he handles his machete like a maniac over there.

However, when he's back at the house, he goes straight to the little ones' hiding place, he gives them treats and plays with them. Then he retires to his bedroom. Mother and I don't dare disturb him.

When he leaves very early the next morning, we pretend we're still asleep.

| Jessica

She sat down in front of me and said:

"Jessica Kamanzi."

Immediately I thought, "That's it. They've finally got me." It was bound to happen one day or another. I had gone around with my face uncovered since the beginning of the massacres, not so much to flaunt it as to protect myself. I wasn't afraid. The fear of death today, for someone like me, would be almost in bad taste. My life isn't worth any more than that of the thousands of people who perish each day.

To buy a little time I pretended I hadn't heard.

"Who did you say you're looking for?"

She repeated my name. I withstood her gaze.

There was something infernal about her beauty. The kind of woman who arouses in men desire, fear, crazy dreams of beginning a new life, and a vague feeling of frustration. She was really stunning. I didn't know her. While I was wondering what attitude to adopt, she said very fast, in a staccato voice:

"I know who you are and what you're doing in Kigali, but I haven't come here to talk about that."

"Excuse me, but I don't know you," I said, cautiously.

"That's not important, Jessica. I just want to tell you that I slept with the priest last night."

I almost screamed:

"What priest?"

As a matter of fact, I knew very well who it was all about. In Kigali, during these days of folly, everyone knew.

Nevertheless, I refused to give myself away. We're dealing with people who are ready to do just about anything. They would be so happy finally to get a spy from the RPF, after they've been talking about it for so long.

"And so?" I said in an offhand way, "I don't really see how that concerns me."

"You work for the RPF in Kigali and only your movement can put an end to this chaos. I hope you succeed."

She was apparently sincere.

"But why come to me to tell me about it?"

"Because you're a good person, Jessica Kamanzi."

"Ah . . . "

"It's also because I want to die."

I kept up my guard, but something about her touched me.

"Every one of us is trying to survive what is happening. Don't let yourself be beaten."

She took her time to say, with gravity:

"Have you taken a good look at me, Jessica Kamanzi?"

She kept pronouncing my whole name, which I found disconcerting.

"I'm too beautiful to survive. I'm as beautiful as the sun, and like the sun there's nowhere for me to hide. They won't believe their eyes when they see me walking peace-fully down the street."

Yes, that young woman had an almost supernatural beauty. It took away any chance she had of escaping the killers. They were going to rape her a thousand times before they killed her. She knew it, and she was going out of her mind.

"The presence of this unknown woman at my side puts me in danger, but I like the light that emanates from her in these days of horror," I thought.

Her story. So commonplace . . . She had found refuge in one of the rare churches in Kigali—perhaps the only one—where, for reasons unknown to me, no mass massacre had taken place. But every night the Interahamwe come with a truck and take away dozens of people to kill them.

"The priest blackmails the people who are there," she says. "He sends the women who refuse to sleep with him to their death."

"And . . . "

I was going to say something stupid. I stopped myself just in time.

I imagined all those girls dying of fright, making up their haggard faces in front of the mirror to seduce the priest. I was so angry! But what gives me, Jessica, the right to judge? I don't know what I would have done in their place.

"I refused for as long as I could," declared the unknown woman.

The priest begged her to take his word for it, he swore that he loved her, asking her to forget what was happening.

"Sometimes he would tell me softly, 'After all this is over, we'll leave. . . . '"

Last Wednesday, four days ago that is, he told her in a

threatening voice as he undressed: "If you keep up this little game I'm going to hand you over to the Interahamwe. I'll ask them to reserve the special treatment for you."

"You know what that means, Jessica Kamanzi? You know how they rape women?"

Yes, I had seen it. Twenty or thirty guys on a bench. Some of them old enough to know better. A woman, sometimes just a frail child, is stretched out against a wall, legs spread, totally unconscious. These good family men aren't into violence. It had chilled my blood to see them chitchatting right at the moment when a whole life was coming apart under their very eyes. And among the rapists there are almost always, by design, some who have AIDS.

"I know how they do it," I said.

"When they've finished, they pour acid in your vagina or stick in pieces of broken bottle or pieces of metal."

"Yes."

I had spoken very quickly. I was ashamed to hear such things.

"I didn't want to suffer, that's why I gave in to the priest."

"Yes."

That day, she had seen in the priest's eyes that he wasn't joking.

"You understand Jessica, I didn't want to die. They take all those people away in their trucks to cut them into pieces."

"That's exactly the problem," I said to myself. "In the worst human tragedies, there are always survivors and everyone thinks that a little bit of luck or cowardice is enough to be one of them."

"I swear to you that I understand," I said to the unknown woman.

I wanted to call her by her name.

She painted me an obscene description of her relations with the priest. He had shaved her pubic hair, taking his sweet time, his gaze mad with desire. He remained hypocritical even in his depravity. He wanted to make her say that she consented.

She stopped talking for a moment and then declared:

"He repeated to me over and over again that he had never seen a woman like me and that after the war against the Inyenzi I would be surprised by the immensity of his love."

I stopped my visitor with a gesture of my hand.

"What's your name?"

"I have no name. I'm the one who's going to die."

"But you're telling me intimate details, it's not worth going into every detail."

"Oh yes it is!" she said vehemently. "Oh yes it is! I don't want to die with that secret."

"People usually say, 'I don't want to live with that secret,'" I thought again. I felt my anger returning. Why was the entire world so indifferent?

She lowered her voice:

"He locked the door so no other noise could enter the room. After filling some wine glasses he put on some soft music, white people's music, and he started to talk about his life and the great career he could have had as a basketball player. Jessica Kamanzi, that man is insane. When he asked me if I liked my job with the little insurance company, I suddenly understood everything. I knew that men sometimes confided the salvation of their souls to demented people. His gestures, which were so perfectly ordinary, betrayed his profound mental derangement. And I, so tired of everything, Jessica Kamanzi, in the middle of the night I told him, as I stroked his hair, that I loved him. And he burst into tears. He cried like a lost child. We made love. The next morning I fled."

I was supposed to answer her. But what could I say? That even greater suffering awaited her during the hours of life that were left to her? The city floated between life and death and the Interahamwe, dressed in tree bark and banana leaves, passed below the window crying like hyenas. They shouted in chorus, at the top of their lungs: "*Tubatsembatsembe*! *Tubatsembatsembe*!" One thing was clear: they didn't want a single survivor. We heard them, she and I. We knew that those cries were the moment's only truth. The rather dismal days of hope were far away. I couldn't even lie to her.

She got up. Her legs were trembling with fear. She leaned on a chair to hide it from me.

"You are winning the war," she said in an admiring tone of voice.

It was true. Towns were falling one after another. We had already secured a large part of Kigali. Government troops were fleeing all over the place at our approach.

"It will also be your victory."

How I wanted to know her name!

She smiled.

"I will be the sun. From up there I'll have my eye on you, you the Rwandans. Join together. Aren't you ashamed, children of Rwanda? Whether someone is Hutu, Tutsi, or Twa, what is it to you? Then, after this awful business is over, behave yourselves and be united, won't you?"

In reality, she was already speaking to us from another world. The stranger was like both a madwoman and a little girl. I had fallen under her charm. I told myself that I would never be able to see the sun again without thinking of her.

She left. I went with her in spirit. In the end, only she

knew why she had behaved that way. But her gesture could not be completely devoid of meaning. Against stupid, wretched, petty killers, almost innocent by dint of being so pitiful, she would say, during her brief journey across the city, the triumphant brilliance of life and of youthfulness.

All that is absolutely unbelievable. Even words aren't enough. Even words don't know any more what to say.

Rosa Karemera

Yesterday morning I thought my time had come. At my age I couldn't run like the others. In addition, there was this awful barricade a few yards from my house. For several days now, the Interahamwe have been performing all their dirty business there. I knew that Valérie Rumiya, a Hutu woman who lives at the other end of our street, had almost gone crazy from the beginning of this mess. She's always hated me—because, she claims, I always look down on everyone, I never say hello, I act like a grand lady, etc. She went from barricade to barricade to ask the Interahamwe: "And that Rosa Karemera, are you quite sure you've killed her?" Finally, she was bothering everyone, and so to get rid of her the Interahamwe answered, "Of course, Mama, that's been taken care of." Then she tried to catch them out: "Tell me what Rosa Karemera looks like, and I'll know if you're telling me the truth! Come on, tell me you little liars!" The Interahamwe, caught off guard at first, didn't know what to reply, then they burst out laughing. Quite a case, this Granny Valérie. They tried to reassure her: "But Mama, there's no way of knowing, we've killed so many people! No Inyenzi from this neighborhood has had the time to run away!" In spite of that, she didn't trust them and continued to ask the same question all over the place.

Her idea of a genocide, that bitch, is just that: to get me, Rosa Karemera, killed. I can't even stick my nose out. So the day before yesterday, through a superhuman effort, I jumped over the wall and landed in the house of my Hutu neighbors. The father, panic-stricken at first, told me that he didn't want to have any problems with the government, then he allowed me to stay. A good man, really, who listened to his heart. But that pest of a Valérie Rumiya found out and gave me away.

Then a soldier from the presidential guard—a warrant officer, I think—arrived. He was really angry. He said, "Here in Butare, you're creating too many problems. You think you're smarter than everyone else just because you have a university here. You hide Inyenzi. If you don't turn in the woman who's in this house, I'll spray you all." He drew a sort of semi-circle with his rifle. Ah! These young people are having a fine time these days. We were lined up in the courtyard. I got out of line, I walked up to him dragging my leg—I've limped since birth, polio—and I said, "Here I am, I'm the woman you're looking for." I wasn't scared any more. I wanted them to get it over and done with. He turned toward me, looked at me from head to toe, and immediately I saw how disappointed he was. Valérie Rumiya must have told him that I was one of the spies that the RPF had been infiltrating in the main cities for the past five weeks. He had imagined me to be

arrogant, very tall, beautiful, and, in a nutshell, disturb-
ingly sensual, and there I was, just a poor scrap of an old
woman, crippled besides. The Hutu family who had hidden me were there and everyone looked at him silently.
You could easily see his embarrassment. Then he declared
brusquely, turning the barrel of his gun down toward the
ground: "OK. Give me ten thousand francs for the kids'
beer." They gave him the money and he left. Of course I
had to change hiding place and I hope to survive this
business. Just to see the look on Valérie Rumiya's face
when she runs in to me in the neighborhood.

Doctor Joseph Karekezi

Come what may, I'll have done my duty.

Duty.

A simple word that I'm fond of.

It wasn't an easy day. To gather all the men that I needed for the job I had to go to Butare and from there on up toward Muciro and Rusenge a bit further north.

Thank God, everywhere I go people immediately say with respect, "Ah! It's Doctor Joseph Karekezi," and everything goes quite well. I also had to make contact with the most conscientious groups of Murambi Interahamwe. It's just that there are more and more people showing up at the Polytechnic. As of tomorrow, we'll be needing a hand there. Time is short.

Unfortunately, several times it's become clear to me that our Interahamwe need to be taken into hand very quickly. The first few days they were full of drive but—why hide the truth?—it's clear that they've been slacking up for a while. Among the numerous scenes I've witnessed by chance during my visits to the barricades, one of them strikes me as particularly edifying. I saw with my own eyes a middle-aged man begging the Interahamwe to have done with him. Nothing very complicated: he wanted to join his son in death. Our men, sitting on piles of corpses that were still warm, were drinking their beer and passing around cigarettes, laughing in his face. They were completely drunk. I couldn't stop myself from smiling when one of them said to him mockingly: "Hey! Don't bother us, you over there, baldy, you talk too much, the death office is closed, come back early this afternoon." The man kept insisting. A hard-headed fellow. They chased him away but he would be back the next minute. Weary of the battle, they decided to get rid of the irksome man. The one who looked to me to be the leader of the Interahamwe made a sign to one of his men to take care of him. His subordinate then got into a rage as violent as it was sudden. He screamed, "Me again! It's always me! Why? The others are here drinking beer and you don't tell them anything! I've been killing all day, I'm tired!" At that moment a dog suddenly surfaced from a pile of corpses, a child's foot clenched in its jaws. The man, who had obviously gone crazy a long time ago, muttered as he crept softly toward the animal: "Ah! Ah! What is this I see? But what is it that I'm seeing? It's my Damien, I recognize his shoe!" He started giving all the details about the shop where he had bought the shoe, explaining on the way that he had had to bargain very hard because the seller was an absolute crook. He also talked about how happy his little Damien had been when he got these brand new shoes, about his wife who had grumbled once again because he spoiled the child, the good grades that the kid had always made at school, and everything. Yes, he was completely cracked. While he was running after the dog, the dog, thinking it was a game, frisked about all over the place, waited for him, then ran off to the cheers of the Interahamwe.

Of course I didn't like that scene. I'm neither a monster nor an idiot. But I would be lying if I were to say that it affected me very much. If you're a determined person, it's a question of knowing what you want. We are at war, period. The sadistic way that things sometimes happen is just a detail. The ends justify the means. Nothing else counts. And in any case, we can't go back now.

When the Interahamwe finally saw me, they stopped joking and word spread, "Papa's here." That's their nickname for me. They like me because I've always helped them. They were told that the doctor who has the tea factory secretly gave a lot of money to the cause! I've been on the ground constantly since the beginning of the war and they know, too, that I don't joke about work. And naturally, when I'm in the vicinity they show their zeal. One of them went at the poor man with violent axe blows, dealing with him loudly, calling him a dirty Inyenzi.

I said to them, "I need your entire unit tomorrow in Murambi." The leader promised me that he would make his men rest during the night. I gave him money for the team's transportation and I left.

I haven't been this uneasy since the beginning of these events. The fact of the matter is: *our men are tired.* It was easy to read on the faces of those I saw. Fatigue and weariness. Our Interahamwe had certainly received good training, but maybe we underestimated the physical effort it takes to kill so many people with knives. The ones they want to eliminate don't make things easy for them, understandably. They run, they scream, they hold on to the

Interahamwe's arms, try different ways to bribe them, in short they'll do anything to prolong their existence by two or three miserable minutes. It's absurd, and even mysterious, in a way, this determination to live, but that's how it is. Our enemies refuse to understand the situation: we're not joking and they don't stand a chance. What it boils down to is that they're setting our lads on edge, and every day they diminish their physical potential. They should be getting their strength back at night, but that's exactly when they insist on organizing these huge drinking binges and taking advantage of the girls they put aside during the day. These frustrated souls maybe thought that everything would be over in a very short while. On the contrary, they now have the impression that they have to start all over again with each new day. For some of them the situation is simple: they've killed the Tutsis who, for one reason or another, they hated, and, without daring to say it openly, they'd like to go home. Unless . . . Yes, we have given them a taste of the exhilaration of being alive. And they're nobody's dupe. Instinctively, they know that if everything turns out alright, they'll go back to their hovels and we certainly won't be coming over to drink banana beer with them. The friendly familiarity, the camaraderie between poor and powerful, that will soon be forgotten. A vicious circle. It's no small matter, chaos.

I also got in touch with Colonel Musoni. He had his moment of glory during the Second Republic. Then, having wanted to take everyone for a ride, he found himself relegated to the sidelines. A real piece of trash, Colonel Musoni. A bitter man. He bet on his life, he lost, and now he accuses the others of cheating. But the colonel was waiting for his moment. Since the death of President Habyarimana he has put his officer's uniform back on to go and tell the peasants in the hills: "As you all know, I was in retirement and didn't want to be involved in politics any more, because I'm too honest. But here: I'm the only one that the young people in the government trust to kill the Tutsis. I have come back to put my experience at the service of the country." And it worked. Very quickly, he had made himself indispensable.

Straight away, Colonel Musoni had started to get involved, with a despicable frenzy, in all kinds of trafficking.

He was on the phone when I got there. His feet perched nonchalantly on top of the desk, he was twirling his moustache as he listened. As soon as he saw me through the windowpane, he asked the person he was talking to to call back later. At the same time he leapt from his chair to come and open the door for me. You measure your own power by this kind of detail. Colonel Musoni has heard that somewhere in Paris they think I should be promoted. The colonel, like so many others, I believe, already sees me at the head of the country. It makes him crazy.

I asked him in a deliberately familiar tone to stop this annoying lackey's behavior:

"What can an old friend do for me? I need men for tomorrow."

"I've already given the order, Doctor. We're being assailed from all sides, but your situation is serious."

He knew what was going on at the Murambi Polytechnic.

"I won't keep them long," I said. "I know that your soldiers also have to go to war."

I found him more tense than usual. Ostensibly, he wanted to tell me something. He knew that people in high places listened to me and he wanted to confide in me. I pushed him to unburden himself:

"It's not going too well right now, Colonel, it seems to me."

"No, Doctor. Revolt is brewing among the troops, if one can put it that way. Even some of the officers are declaring that the Interahamwe will just have to fend for themselves, that our men have enough to do with the RPF."

"They could have thought of that earlier, couldn't they?"

Colonel Musoni made up his mind:

"We're heading toward total defeat, Doctor. . . . I'm a military man and I know what I'm saying."

I had just understood, at last, what he was getting at.

Playfully, I slowly added:

"Unless . . . ?"

He raised his eyes toward me.

"Unless our foreign friends intervene."

"You mean the French?"

"Who else can we count on?"

"Hmmm . . . they've already saved us twice."

"I know," said Colonel Musoni. "June 1992. February 1993."

"And you want to count on them again in 1994? The French have better things to do. . . . "

"Not even to force the RPF into power-sharing?"

"As it says in the Arusha accord?"

"It seems like a good idea to me."

"Arusha was taken down in mid-flight, my friend."

"The politicians should be able to handle the affair," insisted the colonel.

The message was clear.

"Yes," I said, vaguely, "the French supported us against the whole world in this business. They should see it through to the end. So where are they then, those politicians that you're talking about?"

The colonel shook his head:

"They've almost all fled, you're right, Doctor. . . . "

The game of cat and mouse was getting more and more exciting.

"So . . . you understand, my friend?"

The colonel took the plunge:

"I know how modest you are, Doctor. But there are some others and . . . and . . . you yourself, Doctor."

I grimaced, purely for appearances. I was no dupe. The colonel was positioning himself. Tomorrow, he would be able to say: at the moment when all anyone was thinking about was saving his own skin, I was at President Karekezi's side, we stood alone in the middle of the storm, we faced the enemies of the Rwandan nation, it's the two of us and no-one else who have saved the country. His big patriotic pipe-dream. It could be very profitable for those who know how to play it.

President Karekezi . . . Hmm . . . An interesting idea after all. Why not?

I felt the greatest scorn for this officer, an opportunist even in the midst of this disaster. The handsome ageing type. Salt-and-pepper hair. Straight, neatly shaven, well-groomed moustache. It seems that he has a little parcel of virgins delivered to him every night. I tried to make the suspense last:

"To be frank, Colonel Musoni, I may very well leave for Zaïre myself. Why wait for the RPF here? Think about it. You yourself say that everything has gone to hell."

I saw him search me with his cunning eyes to figure out the best thing to reply without getting himself too mixed up in things.

"Yes, uuh . . . Yes, why agree to be the sacrificial lamb, right?" he declared with the air of a wily old devil who has already taken his precautions.

Then he added, for my information:

"In any case, it would be best to go and take up combat again elsewhere."

He should be in politics, this Colonel Musoni. A very gifted fellow, in my opinion.

"Thank you for agreeing to help me," I said, getting up. "I've got to go back to the Murambi Polytechnic."

"I went there last night at around eight o'clock. It's funny how confident our friends seemed."

"They've never lacked for anything."

The colonel knew that Nathalie and my two children, Julienne and François, were among the refugees. Nevertheless, we didn't say a word about it.

On the way to the Polytechnic I thought about Julienne and François, and about their mother. It is no one's fault. At the last minute she'll curse me, thinking that I never loved her. That isn't true. It's just history that wants blood. And why would I only spill other people's? Theirs is just as rotten.

At Murambi I found all my charges in great form. I insisted that they be well fed during these ten days. The Polytechnic had ended up with an excellent reputation. It seemed so safe that some fugitives who were already near the Burundian border opted to come back and settle in there. And because at least you could eat when you were hungry, quite a few Hutu pretended to the presidential guards stationed at the entry that they were Tutsis. I ordered them to be let in. Those bastards should die too. It'll be their punishment for having left the others to do the work. And I, having made a youthful mistake that destroyed my entire life, I will never forgive anyone again for spoiling our blood.

The refugees crowd around me, like they do every time I arrive at the school, and welcome me warmly. They all want to thank me. I went to see Nathalie. A room has been made up for her and the children. The refugees treat her like a queen. The good Doctor Karekezi's wife. And they live practically piled on top of each other in the classrooms, but also in the courtyard and even on the steps of the staircases. I told Nathalie again that all this business would soon be over. I kissed Julienne and François.

I will not see them again.

According to a ritual as immutable as it is mysterious, it's right at the moment that I get back to my car that the refugees present me with their complaints. In general, it's a question of little disagreements due to the overcrowding. This morning something rather strange actually happened: a tall young man with a beard violently took me aside. It was so unexpected that I became uneasy. Did he suspect something? In an acerbic tone he complained about the lack of running water at certain times of day. The other refugees were scandalized by such a lack of gratitude. The young bearded man was just like a union man publicly defying the evil factory owner. People never change. I was really beside myself. Our eyes met. There was a strange glow in his gaze. I told him that I would try my best and that everyone should try to be understanding of certain little difficulties which were inevitable in such a situation.

At the moment my driver started, I gazed longingly at the Murambi hill.

Tomorrow I will be there. Shadows in the dawn mist, facing the motionless trees. Screams will go upward toward the heavens. I will feel neither sadness nor remorse. There will be atrocious pain, of course, but only the weak-hearted confuse crime with punishment. Among those vulgar cries, the pure heart of truth will beat. I am not the kind of person who fears the shadows in his own soul. My sole faith is truth. I have no other God. The moaning of the victims is only the devil's ruse to block the breath of justice and prevent its will to be carried out.

| Jessica

I am stunned. Times like the ones we are living in will also give rise to incredible human beings. They've just informed me of the circumstances of the death of Félicité Niyitegeka, a Hutu nun from Gisenyi. An indomitable woman. "They can spin whatever tales they want," she said, "but I will not kill anyone and I will do everything I can to save human lives." She helped Tutsis who were being chased by killers to cross the border into Zaïre. Her brother, who's a colonel in the regular army at Ruhengeri, sent her a secret letter: "I'm begging you, Félicité, you have to stop what you're doing. The Interahamwe know about your activities, and they're going to come to your house." Félicité Niyitegeka replied: "Let them come. I will keep on saving human lives." So the Interahamwe went to find her in Gisenyi. There were forty-three Tutsi there whom she was getting ready to help cross to the other side of the border during the night.

"We're going to kill them," declared the leader of the Interahamwe.

"I want to die with them."

"We won't be doing that. Your brother is one of us. He pleaded with us to spare you."

She repeated:

"I want to die with them."

"We'll give you some time to think. You'll see that we're not here for fun."

In front of Félicité Niyitegeka's eyes they slowly cut up each one of the forty-three refugees with their machetes, inflicting all kinds of tortures on them.

Then they asked her again:

"Do you still want to follow them where they've gone?"

"Yes," she replied simply.

"Then pray for my soul," said the Interahamwe militiaman to Félicité Niyitegeka.

And he slaughtered her with a bullet straight in the heart.

Here is the letter that Félicité left for her brother: "Dear brother, thank you for wanting to help me. But instead of saving my life and abandoning my charges, these forty-three people, I choose to die with them. Pray for us, so that we may be delivered to God, and say goodbye to my old mother and to my brother. When I am with God, I will pray for you. Take care of yourself, and thank you very much for thinking of me."

This interview with my informant—who insisted that everything he had related, including Félicité's letter, was authentic—left me pensive. I didn't know exactly what to think of it. At first I had a feeling of hope. "Not everything is lost," I told myself, "in the end, we can still become a country like any other. Happy or overwhelmed by misery, I don't know any more. A country like any other, that's all." But then I thought of the thousands of Rwandans, including occasional clergymen, who dipped their hands in the blood of innocents. Could Félicité's gesture make us forget, tomorrow, the ignoble behavior of so many others? After the victory, inevitably, the question will be asked: What is forgiveness worth without justice? The organizers of the genocide know all too well. They are fleeing, and their flight will shelter them from a trial that would heal our people of their trauma.

It will be difficult for those who suffered so much to make allowances for things, to forget the worst to remember only the best. It's easy to calculate the distress of the person who says, "You want me to forgive, but do you know that on Nyanza Hill my seven children were thrown live into a toilet pit?" If he adds: "Think of the few seconds when those children were suffocated by masses of excrement before dying, think just of those few seconds and nothing else," no one will know what to say to him. Will it be enough then, to calm this suffering, to think of the martyrdom of Sister Félicité Niyitegeka or the risks that other anonymous Rwandan citizens took? That, only the future will tell.

For now, the certainty of their defeat is making the killers crazy with hatred. They are becoming more and more cruel. They often force mothers to crush their own babies before being executed themselves. Exactly three days ago, at the Murambi Polytechnic School, in the southeast, Doctor Joseph Karekezi—sadly, the father of a childhood friend in exile in Djibouti—set his killers on thousands of people that he claimed to be protecting. Could it be that his wife and two children were among the victims, as I've been told? I'm waiting for confirmation without much hope: it would be quite in line with the abnormal order of things. Their new credo seems to be reduced to this: we can't eliminate all of them, but the survivors can at least be dead with sorrow for the rest of their lives.

Not having succeeded in getting rid of all the Tutsis, now they're saying that every Hutu must kill. It's a second genocide, through the destruction of souls this time. Lots of ordinary citizens went to it joyfully. It makes for a more lively and colorful infamy, but not more tolerable. And it's not easy for everyone. You should see these decent family men at work. They were not at all prepared for what was expected of them. If they don't yell out they'll never succeed. I understand their strange furor. All their screams are meant to give vent to their innocence: "I'm not killing the Other in order to seize his possessions, no, I'm not so small-minded, I don't even hate him, I'm killing the Other because I'm completely mad, and the proof, it's that the torture I inflict upon him is unique in the history of human suffering."

The result is tens of thousands of putrefying bodies strewn all over the streets, places of worship, and public buildings. A few passersby carry home some armchairs or televisions stolen from the victims. Youths drive around at breakneck speed in cars that don't belong to them. Armed gangs are more and more numerous and anarchical, but the fervor of the first few days has diminished. It's no longer like the beginning when they didn't want to understand anything. Back then, at the barricades, only the very luckiest ones could negotiate their death with an Interahamwe. They would tell him: I'll give you such and such a sum of money and in exchange, you'll kill me with a gun and not with a machete. This care for dignity had a big price then. Now, the Interahamwe are easily corrupted. For almost nothing they'll let you off with your life. They know that it's finished. The leaders think only of leaving the country. The barricades that they haven't had time to take down yet are almost all deserted. But from time to time, on a street corner, you hear laughter and a joyful clapping of hands. A Tutsi that they've discovered by chance. Who came out from his hiding place too soon. They liquidate him as they go. Like a cockroach adventuring out into the middle of the courtyard and blinded by the light. They crush him under the heel of their shoe without paying any attention to him.

Colonel Étienne Perrin

Doctor Karekezi stood aside to let me enter, then closed the heavy iron gate to his house.

"I was waiting for you, Colonel Perrin. . . . Welcome."

His tone was friendly. He held his hand in mine for a moment, no doubt to show some kind of affinity with me. But in this banal gesture I detected a man sure of himself and used to being obeyed.

A long path led up to his apartments. It was lined with bushes that I had never seen before either in Rwanda or in any neighboring countries. The doctor explained to me that he had had them sent from North Africa. He took care of them himself. He liked that; it was a way of relaxing after his hard days at his tea factory or in his office.

"Shall we sit in the garden?"

"Yes, it's a beautiful evening," I replied.

We stood for a moment on the lawn, beside the tennis

court of his sumptuous estate. Sculpted thuja-wood chairs surrounded a low marble table.

"We met each other before briefly, I believe," he said, inviting me to sit down.

That was true. I had appealed to him when we decided to set up the Gikongoro Operation Turquoise headquarters in the Murambi Polytechnic School. There were thousands of bodies all over the place. He gave orders to make them disappear. The Interahamwe dug immense pits to bury the bodies right there. A hell of a job. But everything went well.

"I am happy finally to be able to thank you in person for your help, Doctor."

"It's nothing. . . . "

I was struck by his deep and somewhat drawling voice. He offered me some whisky and got up to go and fetch it from inside the house. I stared after him, thinking with almost ridiculous alarm, given my duty, "So here he is, the famous Butcher of Murambi." He seemed like a normal man. Maybe it's only in movies that killers really look like killers. I certainly wouldn't say that Doctor Joseph Karekezi was an ordinary man. Tall, massive, a little balding, he carries his head haughtily and has a mistrustful look. During the course of my career I have often met human beings who have been called on to make difficult decisions on behalf of others. They see traps everywhere and all have the same worried look, morose and somewhat weary. Doctor Karekezi belonged to this special category, but nothing would make one suspect him of being a hateful and fanatical individual.

He came back with slow steps, balancing a tray on his right hand.

"Ice, Colonel?"

"Yes. Thank you."

He served himself a Coke and thought that he should apologize for it:

"There are two things that I've missed out on in life: alcohol and Saturday night dances. I was always the studious type, and a trifle shy. When I decided to start drinking and dancing it was too late. Cheers, Colonel Perrin!"

"Cheers!" I said in return, wondering what we could possibly be drinking to.

Nothing, evidently. We had on our hands a genocide of unprecedented savagery and a humiliating military defeat. And in any case, I wasn't sure that I wanted to clink glasses to anything at all with Doctor Karekezi. He awoke in me the sort of repugnance and fascination one feels in the presence of sadistic murderers they talk about in the newspaper.

But on the other hand, I had some respect for his courage, which came very close to recklessness. In the midst of the debacle, he was one of the very few people to have lost neither his dignity nor his head. I know what I'm talking about. As of a few days ago my job has been primarily to evacuate ministers, prefects, and superior officers to Bukavu. These gentlemen have only one thing in mind: not to be here when the RPF arrives. They helped themselves to the reserves in the Central Bank and carried away or destroyed the administration's documents and possessions. Seeing their leaders take flight, hundreds of thousands of citizens are also leaving the country for Zaïre, Tanzania, or other neighboring countries. It's an incredible sight, to see all this destitution unleashed onto the roads. For once, I'm in complete agreement with our journalists: this is the most massive exodus of modern times.

As for the doctor, he has a touch of the heroic captain

who refuses to abandon the deck during the shipwreck. He seems to be oblivious to the danger. Each time we spoke to each other on the phone, I only sensed in him vexation and especially anger at the governmental army. At no time did he seem to me to be panicked or simply worried. He knows that he has nothing more to do in Murambi and that from one moment to the next, enemy soldiers could knock down his door and seize him. But instead of thinking of taking shelter, he did his utmost to take the situation in hand. Besides, it's simple: if he hadn't been there, we wouldn't have found anyone to talk to.

"You'll be leaving too, Doctor, won't you?" I asked.

"I'm not playing the brave guy, you know, Colonel Perrin. I'm going to leave, and the sooner the better."

"Butare will fall in a few hours. Probably tomorrow afternoon. You don't have much time to get ready."

"You're telling me? I know all too well that there's nothing else to hope for."

He was quiet for a few seconds, his gaze lost in emptiness, a vacant air about him. Then, turning the glass of Coke around in his hands, he raised his eyes toward me:

"These days I often think about a man in Musebeya who behaved in such an astonishing way: in April, right when our operations started, he put on his best clothes and sat down in his living room with the doors wide open. And there he peacefully awaited his end. The militia arrived, and the man died without so much as a shout. I must say that our Interahamwe in Musebeya were very impressed, they couldn't stop telling the story. . . . "

"And what did they think of it?"

The doctor made a face in which I sensed a mixture of affection and contempt for the Interahamwe:

"They are simple people, Colonel, the meaning of the

gesture escaped them. For them he was just the perfect Tutsi: understanding enough to allow himself to be eliminated without too much fuss."

After a pause he added, amusedly:

"Did you know that in Ruhengeri they ran after their victims, victims they knew very well besides, begging them to stop so that they could kill them more easily?"

"And yourself, Doctor, what do you think of that man's behavior?"

He laughed softly. A sort of ironic chuckle.

"If this isn't an interrogation, it's starting to look like one, isn't it?"

But seeing that he had put me on the spot, he hastened to rectify the situation:

"I'm joking, Colonel. I believe that in spite of everything I have a respect for the fellow. I would like to be able to do what he did, but I have no desire to die."

"Ah?"

I was almost relieved to find myself finally on familiar ground. A man who's afraid of death, at least I know what that means.

"Yes," insisted the doctor, "I want to keep on fighting."

I lit a cigarette. His dog came and lay down at his feet.

"What breed is it?"

"An Appenzeller."

"I know that as a type of cheese."

"He comes from the same place, the canton of Appenzell, in German-speaking Switzerland. Hence the name."

"You had him brought from there?"

After nodding irritatedly, he said:

"We can also talk politics, I think. You know my position. There's no question of leaving the country to these people."

There was no doubt about it. Doctor Karekezi wanted to

know just how far we were prepared to go. What could I tell him? I was hardly more informed than he. In Paris, confusion had reached a peak. Certain enthusiasts already saw us going at it with the RPF resistance fighters in the streets of Kigali, to sort this business out one on one. Others were saying: "We've messed around enough, that does it." According to the camp who were going to take it to Paris, I could order my men to strike on Kigali or to be filmed with Tutsis snatched out of the claws of the terrible Interahamwe. We'll see. I came with my heavy battery of 120mm Navy mortars and Jaguar fighter-bombers, but also with tons of cartons of powdered milk. . . . But I think that the Butare incident is going to weigh heavily on our politicians' decisions. Yesterday, one of our convoys was immobilized by guerrilla forces on the road to Butare: twenty-five of our military vehicles inspected one after the other by RPF forces. We had to let them do it. The slightest move, and we'd have all had it. A kind of humiliation. But there's obviously no question of talking to Doctor Karekezi about that.

To speed things along I said, "If you've decided to go to the northwest, I'm at your disposal. We'll have to leave tomorrow morning."

"That's not what I'm talking about. I'm sure that you've understood me, Colonel Perrin."

"Completely. Only I'm not the one to make decisions. I don't know what we're going to do yet."

"No idea?"

"None."

"Perfect. You're walking out on us because we've gone a bit too far? Well, we'll continue the fight, without you."

I merely nodded my head. At this point in the discussion, silence was my best ally. All the same, I sensed not the shadow of a doubt in the doctor's resolve. He was not the kind to speak idly. The only thing he was concerned about was reversing the situation by all means necessary.

Consequently, I understood a little better why Doctor Karekezi had such fervent supporters among the French who were in charge of the "Rwandan case" as they call it. Before the events, his name had often come up in conversations. He had the perfect profile. A rich and influential Hutu doctor, married to a Tutsi woman, he had become renowned throughout the years for his struggle against impunity in Rwanda. On several occasions he had publicly denounced the massacre of Tutsis. They had thrown him in prison and tortured him, and his family had always lived in danger. One of his sons had lived in exile in Djibouti for years. Habyarimana rather feared him, knowing that in certain influential circles we supported him. Then the doctor had suddenly stopped being interested in public life. This withdrawal gave him the image of a man of good will, prickly yes, but with too much integrity to develop a taste for political games. In short, he could be seen as a recourse for the country and an alternative to a Rwandan president who had got somewhat out of his depths since the beginning of the Arusha talks.

Doctor Karekezi's Parisian partisans were fully aware of his secret activities. They knew what dubious trafficking went on in his tea factory. But he was all the more attractive to them because of it: the man could advance concealed for a long time. Only one thing had not been anticipated: Doctor Karekezi's sensational return to politics, the planned liquidation of forty-five thousand people in Murambi—including his wife and his two children. It was rather embarrassing. But maybe worse was needed to put him out of the game definitively. The Parisian strategists kept scratching their heads: so, Doctor Karekezi or no? Some of them said: "Alright, he's a real bastard. And afterwards? Had they forgotten that in Africa political questions get resolved everywhere with extreme cruelty?"

"Besides," they added, "the survivors of this alleged genocide were soon going to forget the entire episode."

In spite of everything, some more experienced men continued to express their bafflement: this Doctor Karekezi, could he be trusted? He has a strange character, he's unpredictable and one day he'll be out of control. They will retort: "Bah! We've got him, ever since this Murambi business." And the experienced men will drop, with a smile full of hidden meaning, "The Murambi massacre? My dear fellow, maybe he's the one who's got us, after this dirty business. . . . "

So, Doctor Karekezi or no? In high places the position was: no total victory for the RPF. In other words: let's force the winners to accept a power-sharing arrangement with the losers. It was all the more difficult since they no longer knew who they could count on. What cards did they hold again? Doctor Karekezi, in spite of it all? Someone else? But who?

Waiting to come up with a better idea, they assigned me to get Joseph Karekezi across the border and above all to maintain contact with him. It's a mission like any other, and I carry it out dispassionately. I should say, though, that I always feel more comfortable away from Paris. I'm always a bit thrown off by these men with a one-track mind: "Africa is ours, we're not going to let it go." They're all rather crazy over there. They create African heads of state there in their offices. And the latter call late at night to grumble, to beg, to moan: that no-good opponent who's dragging me in the mud and I can't do anything about it you think that's par for the course with your bullshit about human rights yes but in your country does the radio say that the president gave his wife AIDS, oh là là did he really say that, I'm going to give him a talking to there are limits and he's gone too far and then you French people it's promises and promises and we never see anything my government's still waiting for its credit for the second university yes it's true the file is making the rounds let's say a few more months but no sir I can't say whether it will be before or after your re-election frankly I can't say yes goodnight to you too thank you good-bye Mister President. And bla bla bla and when there's someone in the office you say excuse me I was with President Whatchamacallit it's my daily lot my way of the cross oh sweet Jesus who'll save me from the Saviors of the Homeland. . . .

I noticed that the least resilient of them ended up becoming racists. Knowing of Africa only their distant and docile creatures, chosen precisely for their mediocrity, they get to be convinced, even if they can never say it out loud, that Africa is pure shit. And that's why they believed, in nicknaming the RPF fighters the "Khmer Noir," they would turn the whole planet against them. Another act of stupidity. Nothing has gone right for us in this Rwandan affair. In the Parisian ministries right now, their hearts are sinking. There are all these journalists and human rights defenders who weren't exactly part of the plan. The upshot: an Operation Turquoise that lots of people are laughing at. To play the kind soul after letting our protégés commit all these stupid atrocities! No one's been fooled. The proof: only Dakar—as usual—has gotten involved. No one else wanted to send troops.

"Listen, Doctor," I said, "I respect your refusal of defeat. . . . However, during these last three months your army has given up fighting. Military man that I am, I find that hard to fathom."

"I know," said Doctor Karekezi, pulling on his dog's collar, "I know, yes . . . they're hopeless."

He had no desire to discuss that topic.

I insisted: "Was it really more important to kill all those unarmed people than to fight the RPF?"

I saw something light up in his eyes and he said, with a studied slowness, his right thumb pointing downward, "The truth, Colonel, is that you either have them or you don't. And you didn't."

"Excuse me?"

"You didn't have the balls."

Frowning, I sat up straight. At that precise moment I felt I was dealing with the real Doctor Karekezi, not the one who up to then had spoken to me in a disabused and courteous manner.

"Take back what you just said, Doctor."

My voice was both calm and tense, and somewhat menacing. What he had just said was insulting, and I didn't intend to let it go.

Pleased at having achieved the desired effect, Doctor Karekezi said carelessly, "Of course, I'm not talking about you, Colonel Perrin. . . . "

"I would like an apology, please."

He saw that I wasn't joking. The atmosphere was starting to deteriorate. Coolly, he said, "Well, my sincere apologies. I thought I could take the liberty with a fighter such as yourself. Let's just say, then, that our friends didn't dare carry their plan through to its logical conclusion."

"And do you think you helped them?"

"I know the story. The band of Kigali murderers. You've suddenly discovered that we're not the kind of people you should be associating with, is that it? . . . You didn't know. . . . The perfect pretext . . . Everything took place in broad daylight. The radio warned the killers: 'Hey, what kind of bad work is this? A band of Tutsis about to cross into Tanzania have been spotted near Nyarubue. Hurry up, fellows, let's move it.' You had this country under your control, Colonel. You knew every nut and bolt of the killing machine and you looked away because it suited you."

Despite the harshness of his words, Doctor Karekezi had expressed himself calmly, never stopping from gently tugging the animal's collar.

In a purely professional reaction I thought, "This man is truly dangerous." He was a real desperado, not at all the type to let himself go without reacting. Maybe it was better not to get on his bad side. Besides, I was having trouble disagreeing with him. I was of almost the same opinion as him.

I remembered Jean-Marc Gaujean. A young man in the ministry, quite idealistic and tormented, who likes to confide in me. We were having a coffee at the Mandoline, in the eleventh arrondissement. He seemed worried. "That business again, my friend?" I said, touching his arm. "Yes, it stinks. They're going to keep talking about it, Rwanda here, genocide there, and every day they'll pull a new cadaver out of the cupboard." He added, "It's not our fault." "No," I replied, "it's the fault of the Rwandans themselves. They need to cope with this enormous bloodstain in their history. To say otherwise would be to think of them as irresponsible children. But, Jean-Marc, we did nothing to prevent the massacres. We were the only ones in the world who could have done it." I slid my finger along my left arm and said, "My dear Jean-Marc, we're in blood up to here in all of this." That was the very evidence, he knew it. Shaking his head he said, "And here we are, required to help killers escape justice in their own country. . . . It's a terrible process, but it's our only option. If there's a trial, they can try and save their skins by putting everything on us. We're literally stuck." Then he asked me the question that he felt so strongly about: "Certain comparisons are exaggerated in any case, don't you think?" We both knew what he was alluding to. I've rarely met such a pure person: he thought neither of a continent nor a race, but of millions of shattered human lives. That was refreshing. Hundreds of people around me loudly proclaim their love for Africa, which always makes me a bit suspicious: they want people to admire its merits because they think they need all they can get to respect such a despicable continent. In the end, Jean-Marc wanted me to reassure him. I couldn't bring myself to do it. "A genocide is a genocide," I answered, "and this one will be the same. The more time passes, the less we'll forget." We had the same stretch of metro to take on the Balard-Créteil line close by. Jean-Marc said to me, just before getting off at the Richelieu-Drouot stop, "It's bizarre. If you go, you'll be working with the doctor who organized the massacre in the school?" "Yes," I replied, "And between you and me, Jean-Marc, I'm anxious to see what kind of person he is." "See you tomorrow, Étienne," he said. We had a meeting about Operation Turquoise at the ministry the following day. Jean-Marc disappeared down an escalator into the Parisian crowd, and I imagined him on a visit to Rwanda. A face-to-face between Jean-Marc Gaujean and Doctor Karekezi. He'd never get over it. A good history lesson for that young civil servant still concerned with virtue.

While I was conjuring up these memories, the doctor was satisfied to look at me, watching my reaction.

"You just said, Doctor, that these killings suited us. I don't quite see how."

He twisted his mouth somewhat condescendingly. Obviously, he had been waiting for the question.

"Over there, in Paris and in your army, too many people ended up feeling as much hatred as us for the RPF. Shady characters from other places. You don't check them. They speak English and they look down on you. It's the last straw, isn't it? Blacks who don't kowtow to you. Hatred, you can handle that, but this indifference, no. That's worth killing several hundred thousand Tutsis."

"Not a single Frenchman shed any Rwandan blood," I said, adamant.

He gave a short snigger which caught me completely off guard.

"And me, Colonel Perrin? Look at my hands. Do you think I've ever held a machete? I'm a poor little surgeon. I save lives! I've never spilled a drop of blood either."

"Perhaps we made some mistakes in our assessment of the situation, but we have never killed anyone nor had anyone killed."

I'm not sure whether he's understood me. He said suddenly, in his fascinatingly calm way:

"Besides, they fight really well, these RPF fellows."

"Are you the one who's saying that, Doctor?"

"I'm lucid, dear friend, that's all. By the way, do you know that they've decided not to take the last town, Ruhengeri, until the 14th of July? Isn't that tactless? The 14th of July! That deserves a reaction on your part, doesn't it?"

What a devil of a man! I refused to follow him down the path where he wanted to lead me.

"In my opinion, Doctor, above all you should ask yourself the following question: what if you had it to do all over again?"

"I don't regret anything," he declared immediately. "The journalists and all the riffraff are going to shriek like little girls who are afraid of the dark. I'm going to tell you something that you might not appreciate: for me, the idea that a human life has any worth is pure convention."

"Even your own, Doctor?"

"That's none of your business."

His tone had quickly become sour.

"What a despicable guy!" I thought.

"Well, the truth is, Doctor Karekezi, that you had a mansion built in the eastern part of Zaïre in case the situation got bad here and yet you insult those you sent to their death. That's too facile."

I was beside myself. My rage was even making me tremble. He didn't react.

I hammered in the nail:

"Isn't it true that you own a palace on the shore of Lake Kivu?"

"Correct," he said dryly before adding: "I sent them to their death, but in Murambi your men have built volley-ball courts and installed barbecues on top of mass graves. That's what you call humanitarianism, is it?"

All civility was over. I pointed to the swimming pool, the tennis court, and the rare plants, and I said:

"You're philosophizing, Doctor, but you killed your wife and your two children so as not to lose all these beautiful things. You're not such a special person, Doctor, just a pathetic nouveau riche African. You liquidated all those poor people out of pure greed."

He started drumming his fingers on the arm of his chair.

"First sign of nervousness," I noted with satisfaction, "I've touched a nerve." He had hoped to pass, in my eyes, for the Angel of Death, terrible but just. It had failed. And God damn that son of a bitch, anyway!

"Thank you for your hospitality," I said, pushing my glass out of the way. "I will come and get you myself to-morrow."

"Thank you very much, Colonel Perrin. We'll see."

We stood up. In the end, I knew nothing about this man. I wanted to hurt him and, all too cognizant of the fact that I was dealing with the worst kind of monster, I found him vaguely moving.

I bent down to stroke the dog.

"His name is Taasu," he said without emotion.

"Taasu? A funny name."

"It's not me who gave it to him," clarified the doctor, his face suddenly impenetrable.

"His children must have found it in a comic book. . . . This is all beyond me," I thought.

"I see that Taasu hasn't become aggressive, like . . . like the others."

"You're talking about those dogs that stuffed themselves so full of human flesh during the war that now they attack people?"

"That's what they tell me."

"No," he declared, smoothly, with a little grimace of disgust, "that didn't happen to this dog. Only the dogs in the popular neighborhoods fed on Tutsi cadavers. You're right to think that my Taasu doesn't do that kind of thing."

All the ambiguous charm of the conversation had just vanished. I said stonily, looking him straight in the eye:

"You're playing the cynic because you've lost everything. War criminals always end up beaten."

"Colonel Perrin, we're in the same boat. What happened in Rwanda is, whether you like it or not, a moment of French history in the twentieth century. Just imagine, I'm not an amateur: I'm fully aware of what happened to your convoy in Butare, yesterday at dawn. You had asked Dallaire, the Canadian general, to warn the RPF commanders that it was absolutely forbidden to enter Butare; you would not allow it. You were putting on your Great

Power act. The RPF guys answered, 'Oh yeah? We'll see about that.' And they did. That had never happened to you before. It's the beginning of the end, my dear friend. You'll leave Africa by the back door."

I couldn't miss such an opportunity to remind him of his miserable situation. I asked him disdainfully, a smile on my lips:

"And you, Doctor, will you leave your country tomorrow at dawn or not? I need an answer."

"I'll see you tomorrow, Colonel Perrin. If I understood right, you are . . . shall we say . . . obliged to evacuate the war criminal to Bukavu? Orders from my good friends in Paris, is that right?"

"Wait for me in the courtyard, please. That's all. Your wild imagination doesn't interest me."

The doctor smiled:

"Come in any case. But it's possible that I might refuse to go, just to get you in trouble."

I didn't have the time to answer. He closed the door softly.

But I knew I would find him ready. He's a coward. Only a coward could behave the way he did at the Murambi Polytechnic.

| Jessica

Kigali is once and for all in our hands. The massacres have stopped. On Saturday and Sunday we took control of the airport and the Kanombé camp before surrounding the presidential palace. I found out this morning that the towns of Gitarama and Kabgayi have also fallen. At this pace, it will all be finished by the third week in July or even earlier.

These last few days people have been talking a lot about a French military intervention. How can a great country abandon its friends in difficulty? Paris would like to do something. Just to force us to a compromise with their longtime allies. But those allies have, so to speak, raised the bar too high. They haven't realized that their spectacular barbarity was in fact a political liability. As for us, we're ready for any sacrifice to defend such a hard-earned victory.

Any way you look at it, the situation is so bad for their men that the French have thought it more prudent to wait and see. Two thousand five hundred of their soldiers, heavily equipped, are taking up position in Goma and Bukavu in Zaïre. They're calling it Operation Turquoise. It seems to be a matter of coming to the aid of Tutsis threatened by the genocide. We'll see how they manage to save the lives of people who've been dead for such a long time. It's all a really sinister farce.

All the same, the losers have had the time to regain their hope. In the few areas of the country where they can still move around freely, the Interahamwe go back and forth through the streets crying, "Vive la France!" When foreign troops pass by, they heartily applaud them.

The free radio and television station Mille Collines announces, "My Hutu sisters, make yourselves pretty, the French soldiers are here, now's your chance, because all the Tutsi girls are dead!"

PART FOUR | *Murambi*

At the end of the footpath a wooden fence cut across the high grass bending slightly in the wind. The air was dry and the sky pure. On his right, a few yards from where he was standing, Cornelius made out a tiny building with a tin roof and filthy cracked walls.

The house where he was born.

Despite his efforts, he could not find the front door. He stood still for a few minutes, turning his head this way and that as if to catch, in the heart of the silence, an echo of the past. He stood waiting for the clear laughter of children who would say to him in a familiar tone, "Ah, it's you, Cornelius Uvimana, here you are, back again. We've been waiting for you for such a long time." Or even, rising up suddenly from all around, the screams of terror, just as in those nights when strangers came to pillage, burn, and kill. That was, after all, the flesh and blood of his exile. He knew why the house was empty. And yet, it was painful for him to admit that it was also dead to his memory. Had the dead carried off his childhood, leaving him nothing in exchange but their names? No face emerged clearly from his memory.

As a teenager in Bujumbura he used to see refugees arriving with bad news every day. He, Stan, and Jessica already formed a little gang. They listened to the grownups talk about massacres in Rwanda. They said, "Eleanor Mwenza, Siméon's wife, was raped by some kids." Aunt Eleanor who always went to church in a blue dress? Yes, they remembered the name, but they could not remember exactly who she was. Siméon was out in the fields. "They watched her put out the fire by herself, and then they did their dirty work on her before they killed her." Another day they learned that there was no one from Siméon's family left in Bugesera.

In Djibouti, too, he received letters. His cousin, Gaëtan, Aunt Rosalie's son, did he remember him? No, he did not. It was an epoch when time staggered backwards, drunk with hatred. Death came before life. And later, Murambi. His mother, Nathalie. He hardly knew her either. In his mind floated the image of a small woman, slightly round, self-effacing, and of delicate health. Julienne and François. The brother and sister born after his departure.

After a moment's hesitation, he slipped in through the half open fence to get to the house. The rear wall was so close that he almost hit his forehead on it. In the middle of the courtyard he passed alongside a furrow that had no doubt been dry for some time. The only noise he heard was that of his own footsteps on the dead leaves.

Tufts of grass sprang from a cracked section of the wall. Untidy vines wound around the tree trunks. Everything was growing in a sort of wild outburst.

Cornelius headed toward the place where the animal pen used to be. That's where Siméon's bulls had been burned alive.

He couldn't forget that.

He had often relived the moment in his mind. He was arriving in the evening to a sleeping house and was standing in the middle of the courtyard, a bundle set at his feet. Nothing more. The idea of this return to simplicity fascinated him.

"Who are you looking for, stranger?"

The voice came from behind him.

He turned around.

The man, dressed in an old suit of khaki-colored cloth and a red scarf around his neck, was standing against the doorjamb, his two hands leaning on his walking stick. He must have been watching Cornelius in silence during the few minutes he was walking around the courtyard.

"Siméon Habineza . . . " murmured Cornelius without moving.

The name had formed itself alone on his lips.

"Don't you recognize me, Siméon?"

He was almost shocked.

The man smiled mischievously:

"Not recognize *you*, Cornelius Uvimana? Come on, come over here."

They embraced each other without a word. Siméon's look, sweet and somewhat sad, added to the serenity of his face. Hardship had weakened him, he was thin and wrinkled, but a great spiritual force emanated from him.

"So you didn't get off the bus at the station?"

"No. Why?"

"Young Gérard Nayinzira went there to get you."

The name vaguely rang a bell with Cornelius.

"Who is he? I might have met him in Kigali."

"He often goes there. His friends have given him another name. . . . "

"The Skipper?"

"Yes. He dreamed of being a sailor when he was small."

"Ah . . . But we don't have any sea here!"

"So what? Isn't that a real dream? He read lots of books and now he knows all kinds of things about the sea and life on board boats. Gérard is from Bisesero, but now he lives in Murambi. You'll meet him. Let's go inside, I'm going to show you to your room."

The room was very modest: a brown wardrobe with two doors, a big foam mattress placed directly on the floor, whose color hesitated between blue and green. Siméon had also had a worktable and a chair put in the corner on the right.

Cornelius felt intuitively that the room had been closed up for a very long time, perhaps years. He was touched to see that Siméon had fixed it up especially for him. As far back as his memory could go, he had always seen his uncle help others.

Siméon checked that all was in order, gave him some explanations, and went to sit on his mat in the middle of the courtyard. Despite his kindness, his gestures bore a stamp of reserve that commanded respect. In spite of himself, he imposed a certain distance. In his presence, Cornelius had the strange impression of becoming, once again, the twelve-year-old kid who left Murambi for Bujumbura, and then Djibouti.

But maybe one doesn't emerge from exile without becoming a child again. It was so difficult to come back home after twenty-five years of absence without being able to ask anyone for news.

The house was once again plunged into torpor and sadness. To think of Siméon sitting alone, waiting for him in the courtyard, made his heart bleed. He made up a little packet of the presents he had brought and set them next to the pillow. He would give them out later.

He joined Siméon in the middle of the courtyard.

"I have tea from Djibouti," he said, sitting down across from him.

"I've just asked Thérèse to make us some."

"Mine's good too. You'll see."

"I'll prepare that tea myself," said Siméon.

Cornelius saw himself again in the Djibouti market, shopping with Zakya. She had told him, "You've spoken to me so often about Siméon Habineza that I feel as if I know him. I'm going to pick all his presents myself."

He looked all around him and said, pointing to a row of bricks on his right, "That's where the animal pen used to be."

"I saw you head over there a little while ago. Jessica and Stanley also asked me about it once."

"And what did you say to them?"

"That it's good to remember certain things. Sometimes it helps you to find your path in life."

"Which means . . . ?"

Cornelius saw in Siméon's face that he didn't want to expand on the subject. But the old man nevertheless answered:

"That's how we know what trials we had to overcome to merit being alive. We know where we come from."

"Memories are coming back to me, little by little," said Cornelius.

"The house has stayed the same. A family needs that."

A woman—fifty years old or thereabouts—brought them some tea.

"Thérèse, this is Cornelius Uvimana, my nephew. You know him by name. He's come back home."

They greeted each other.

"Is she a relative?" asked Cornelius after Thérèse left.

"No, a neighbor. She takes good care of me."

Their eyes met and Siméon added:

"I know, Cornelius, it's hard to come home after so many years and to think of one's family without even daring to mention them by name."

He stopped talking. Cornelius repeated, like an echo, for himself:

"No, it's not easy, I was just thinking of that."

"But I'd like us to talk about the day when I took you to the shores of Lake Mohazi. Do you remember?"

Cornelius looked at him with emotion:

"I remember that child who played the flute. I've never forgotten him."

"I see that you have a very good memory."

Then Siméon listened to Cornelius tell him how twenty-nine years earlier he, Siméon, had driven him to Gasabo Hill and had said to him, as he showed him the shores of Lake Mohazi with a broad sweep of his hand, "This is where Rwanda was born."

That morning, as his nephew reminded him, Siméon's eyes suddenly became more intense.

Cornelius saw it all again. Beneath their feet, the muddy ground saturated in places with heavy, blackish water. The ragged shepherd driving two or three animals to the watering hole. The bull with long, pointed horns that made a circle above his head. Toward the east, behind Gasabo Hill, a white spot in the sky. And above all, the child with the flute. Cornelius was crushing a guava leaf between his fingers to smell its perfume. At that precise moment the clear, pure sound of a flute rose up toward the sky. A boy of about ten years of age, no doubt the shepherd's son, had passed in front of them without appearing to see them. The scene, which remained vivid in his mind, had nourished his years of exile. Depending on the day, it came back to him in fragments—the slightest detail could then plunge him into a long bout of reverie—or like an almost perfect painting.

"That's what should stay," said Siméon after Cornelius had recounted it.

"That's what I've always thought," said the young man.

"And now, tell me what you've done in that country. . . . "

"In Djibouti? I was a history teacher in a school."

"And what history did you teach the children?"

Cornelius guessed at Siméon's allusion.

"We didn't talk very much about Rwanda."

"What do you mean? Djibouti schoolchildren don't know that God finds our Rwanda so pleasant that he never spends the night anywhere else?" asked Siméon, mockingly.

Cornelius turned toward the lights scattered over the Murambi hill and answered, somewhat disabused, "My pupils wouldn't have believed me. The word Rwanda evokes only blood and endless killings for everyone."

"Every country is the most beautiful in the world," observed Siméon. "I want you to tell me about Djibouti."

At seventy-seven years of age, Siméon had never gone further than Burundi. Cornelius tried to get him to feel how different Djibouti was from Rwanda.

"Over there, you find emptiness everywhere. It's a country that's smaller than ours, but you get the impression that it's never-ending."

What words would he use to describe the reds and blacks of the desert to Siméon?

"The heat there is sometimes terrible. . . . Actually, I'm not able to explain Djibouti. I'll try some other time."

"Maybe it would be easier for you to talk to me about Zakya, then?"

Siméon seemed very amused by Cornelius's amazement.

"Tell me, Siméon Habineza, how is it that you know everything?"

"Your good friends. Jessica told me: 'When Cornelius talks about that young woman from Djibouti, his eyes sparkle!' Listening to you just then I saw that she was right."

Cornelius gave a hearty laugh.

"What are you up to behind my back? I didn't even know that Stan and Jessica had been to see you in the meanwhile."

"Will she come here, Zakya?"

"Yes."

"I like this idea of mixing people from all over the place. Maybe we've kept to ourselves too long here in Rwanda."

"Her name is Zakya Ina Youssouf."

"I have the feeling that if I don't stop you, she's going to make us spend the night outside. That's for tomorrow. It's getting late, let's go and rest. If you need anything, don't hesitate to call Thérèse. She knows what you mean to me."

Once again they crossed the courtyard where an atmosphere of total desolation reigned. Kitchen utensils lay upside down on the ground, and there were no traces of footsteps in the sand. Cornelius could see by his hesitant gestures that Siméon could no longer see very well. But solitude and poverty had not been able to keep the old man down.

When they reached the steps, Siméon said in his most serious manner:

"Cornelius Uvimana?"

"Yes."

"Are you listening to me, Cornelius Uvimana?"

"Yes, Siméon."

"I took you, all those long years ago, to Gasabo because

I knew that one day you would leave. You've come back and difficult moments are awaiting you. You know what has happened, and we suffer a lot, even if we don't show it. Some feel guilty for not having been killed. They wonder what fault they committed to still be alive. But you, try to think about what is yet to be born rather than what is already dead."

Cornelius thought again of the child they had encountered on the shore of Lake Mohazi. The image of a world that nothing could destroy. The image of eternity.

"Good night, Siméon."

"Cover yourself well, the nights can be very cold right now."

"I already noticed that in Kigali," said Cornelius, helping him back to his room.

The young woman in the green blouse was sitting alone on a bench in the hallway.

As soon as she saw the visitor come through the door of the Polytechnic, she pulled on her rubber gloves and slipped into a spacious room.

When he got close to her, Cornelius realized that she was busy arranging human remains. She picked up a tibia and placed it next to others of the same length; she set on a pile of remains a skull that had been left in the middle of the way and sprinkled it all with a white powder with an awful smell. These frighteningly banal gestures and this need for order must be part of the routine of her existence, thought Cornelius. Important people would sometimes come in delegations from far off countries to visit the Murambi Polytechnic. She did her best to receive them properly.

Cornelius had prepared himself for the worst. But his glimpse of the first skeletons behind a window had an unexpected effect on him: he immediately wanted to turn around and go back. These dead people laid out on the ground struck him as very different from the ones he had already seen. In Nyamata and Ntarama time had put the finishing touches to the work of the Interahamwe: skulls, arms, and legs had become detached from their torsos and the different types of remains found there had had to be organized separately. In Murambi, the bodies, which were covered with a fine layer of mud, were almost all intact. Without his being able to say why, the remains in Murambi gave him the impression of still being alive. He took fright. Instead of going into the classrooms, he started pacing up and down the hallway, glancing indecisively in every direction, as if looking for a place to flee. Saliva was collecting in his throat and he swallowed it to conceal his disgust. Even from the outside the stench of the cadavers was intolerable.

A bearded man of about forty, tall and thin in gray trousers and a white shirt, appeared at the back of the courtyard and came toward him:

"May I help you, sir?"

Cornelius looked at him without seeing him.

"I came home from abroad about ten days ago," he said. "My relatives were killed here."

After a moment's hesitation he added:

"My name is Cornelius Uvimana. I am the son of Doctor Karekezi."

He had nothing to hide. Everyone must know what infamous person he was the son of.

But the man seemed not to have heard him. Cornelius followed him, not without noticing that the man hadn't introduced himself.

The Murambi Polytechnic School was composed of seven or eight buildings arranged without any apparent order on a vast lot of several hectares.

The man gave Cornelius detailed explanations. The World Bank had given a grant, he told him, for the construction of the school, but work had been interrupted by the events. The rooms in the back were supposed to serve as apprentices' workshops for the high school students. A bit further, behind the trees, a football field had been planned. He pointed out the buildings and turned toward Cornelius:

"You see, of course, that they didn't have the time to paint the buildings."

And, in fact, the walls were all a sinister gray color.

The man started talking about the massacre:

"During the genocide, a prominent Murambi man gathered thousands of Tutsis here, promising to protect them. Then, when there were enough of them, the Interahamwe arrived and the carnage started."

Cornelius said calmly:

"It's my father who did that."

"I know," said the man, without showing the slightest emotion.

Cornelius wanted to tell the man that what happened was his fault but thought that such a declaration wouldn't make any sense.

"How many people died here?"

"Between forty-five and fifty thousand."

At the entrance to each room the man turned to Cornelius and said:

"There are sixty-four doors like this one. . . . "

And each time Cornelius thought to himself: "The doors of Hell." Was the man expressing himself in such a strange way on purpose?

In this place, amid sorrow and shame, his own life and the tragic history of his country met. Nothing spoke to him of himself as much as these remains scattered on the naked ground. Siméon's words came back to him. He had told him, a few days earlier: "Cornelius, don't regret leaving, because you deserved to live more than anyone." He had asked him why and Siméon had answered: "Because your mother, Nathalie, brought you in to this world running, to escape from the people who wanted to kill her." And that was where his destiny had come full circle: a young woman in labor hiding from bush to bush in Bugesera, and now him, Cornelius Uvimana, standing in the middle of these remains in Murambi. Presently, he could add: "After all, she ended up being killed. By my father. And her body is here. Lost among thousands of others." Nathalie Kayumba. Julienne. François. Pathetic little bits of bone. Yes, he had been right to smile during his discussion with Jessica. In a way, all of this was comical.

But why did these rooms piled with corpses make him think of life rather than of death? Perhaps because of the way their arms were stretched out toward the Interahamwe in a last absurd plea? A forest of arms still murmuring with the cries of terror and despair. He stopped next to a corpse: a man or a woman whose left foot had been cut off at the ankle. What remained of the leg was stiff like a real crutch. He was surprised not to be thinking of anything in particular. He was satisfied to look, silent, horrified.

"Do you want to go on, sir?"

The man must have noticed Cornelius's efforts to brave the nauseating stench of decomposing bodies.

"Yes. I want to see everything."

"You'll see the same bodies everywhere."

"No," said Cornelius dryly, "I don't think so."

He was so furious with the unknown man that he almost asked him to leave him alone. This sudden bout of rage revealed to him his own suffering, much more profound than he had thought.

The man said:

"Yes, you're right. I'm sorry."

Of course he was right. Each one of these corpses had had a life that was different from that of all the others, each one had dreamed and navigated between doubt and hope, between love and hate.

Cornelius understood better now the authorities' decision not to bury the victims of the genocide after the controversy that came up about it in the country. Some people said that they had to be given a decent burial, that it isn't good to exhibit cadavers like that. Cornelius didn't agree with that point of view. Rwanda was the only place in the world that these victims could call their home. They still wanted its sun. It was too soon to throw them into the darkness of the earth. Besides, every Rwandan should have the courage to look reality in the eye. The strong odor of the remains proved that the genocide had taken place only four years earlier and not in ancient times. As they were perishing under the blows, the victims had shouted out. No one had wanted to hear them. The echo of those cries should be allowed to reverberate for as long as possible.

Cornelius sometimes lingered on the faces of very young children. They seemed peaceful, as if they were simply asleep.

They continued the visit. On one body he saw bits of braids; on another, a piece of green cloth; a skeleton was curled up like a fetus: someone who must have resigned himself to death without daring to look it in the face. A skull, lying solitary in a corner, particularly struck him. The victim—surely a giant when he was alive—had had his nose severed before being decapitated. Faint black spots were still visible on his right cheek. A dark line, lightly curved, represented his mouth. It was like a death mask, forgotten in the middle of the other corpses. Or— Cornelius, however, didn't dare let this vaguely indecent idea linger in his mind—a clown with a moon face. It was as if fate had carefully sculpted, according to some mysterious design, this massive and slightly sullen face.

In another room his guide showed him the weapons used by the Interahamwe: sticks, clubs studded with rusty nails, axes and, of course, machetes.

As they were crossing the courtyard in the direction of other buildings, Cornelius suddenly raised his head toward the man:

"How do you know who I am?"

"Everyone in Murambi knows that Doctor Karekezi's son is in town."

Cornelius was silent. That was another story, that. For the moment, he had to concentrate on the dead.

"It seems that there were ten or so survivors. . . . "

"I'm one of them," declared the man.

Cornelius, shocked, turned quickly toward him.

"You didn't say anything to me about it. . . . "

"You didn't ask me anything. My name is Gérard Nayinzira. It's the old man who asked me to get here before you."

"The old man?"

"Siméon Habineza."

"I thought you were the caretaker. I'm sorry."

"You still don't see who I am?" said the man, in turn.

Cornelius understood immediately.

Skipper.

"They call you the Skipper, don't they? We saw each other one night in Kigali."

"Yes, at the Café des Grands Lacs."

"I'm really sorry, Gérard. Please don't hold it against me."

"I understand very well what must be going on in your head right now."

The man showed him an enormous crater in the center of some wild grass:

"There are several of these in this school. These holes served as mass graves."

"I was told that in Murambi the victims were buried, then exhumed," said Cornelius.

"That's correct. The bodies are intact because there's clay in the soil here. Besides, you've noticed that the skeletons are all a bit red."

It was still possible to see, at the edges of the graves, part of the sand that had been loosed when the bodies had been exhumed after the victory of the RPF.

"But who had had them buried?"

"Some French officers with Operation Turquoise."

"Oh, really?"

"Yes. Come with me, I'm going to show you something."

He led Cornelius behind some other, bigger rooms, and had him touch a flagpole put up on top of a little pile of brown pebbles:

"This is where they hoisted their flag. As soon as they arrived in the zone, they saw that this school was just what they needed. But there were cadavers all over the place. A certain Colonel Étienne Perrin asked the authorities to find a solution."

"You mean that he went to my father?"

"Yes. Doctor Karekezi ordered the Interahamwe to place the bodies in these common graves. At that time, the militia weren't taking orders from anyone anymore, but they still had a lot of respect for the doctor, whom they called 'Papa.'"

"I see," said Cornelius.

"The French soldiers lent them the equipment, and when the cadavers were collected in the graves, they set up camp on top of them."

Cornelius, fascinated, speechless with amazement, took a long time to leave the Murambi Polytechnic. He took the tour of the classrooms again. He waited for the bodies to divulge their secret to him. Which one? There was only one, of which, confusedly, he had a premonition.

On the way back Gérard swore to him:

"The other evening, in the Café des Grands Lacs, I was just about to do something really stupid."

"You were holding it against me. It's normal."

"I wanted you dead. It's your father who did it. And you, you weren't there when we were suffering."

"That's what lots of people think, I'm sure, but there's nothing I can do about it. In any case, I appreciate your talking to me so frankly, Gérard."

"I had come to call you, publicly, the son of a murderer. But at the last minute, I remembered Siméon Habineza. He is such a good man. I couldn't do that to him."

Cornelius thought that Gérard would never fully forgive or forget what had happened. For himself, everything had been so easy: he felt that he would never be able to understand the pain that had not been his. His return was almost becoming another exile.

"You were there, in the Café des Grands Lacs, comfortable, sure of yourself, and you didn't know that everyone was following your slightest gesture and listening to your words. People were coming expressly to see, with their own eyes, the son of the Butcher of Murambi, there were some security guys there too, you didn't realize anything."

"There was no way for me to know."

In his heart of hearts he felt irritated by Gérard's accusations, but he didn't dare show it. Gérard was just waiting for the moment to let his rage explode. "He's got me, like an animal with its prey and he won't be letting me go in a hurry," he thought.

"Alright," said Gérard, "but at least know that they're watching you. Always. Never forget it."

"And what have I done then?" shouted Cornelius suddenly.

He had decided to burst open the abscess. He would just as soon hear Gérard call him the son of a murderer than let him play with him so cruelly.

"You started to talk about that pretty girl who gave you the eye in a bar in Abidjan," said Gérard coldly, "You were making big gestures, your entire body was getting away from you, while we, because of circumstances, we've learned to draw in our bodies, we've received so many blows, right? And there, at the GL, the only thing we heard was you, you joked with Franky the waiter, in a word, you felt great. The first day you were rather on guard, you probably told yourself: 'Ah! They've suffered so much, I'd better be quiet,' but you quickly got to thinking that you could still have a good time, genocide or not!"

"You're unfair, Gérard."

In an instant, solely from the intensity of his voice, Cornelius had just realized that Gérard could kill him at any moment.

"Unfair, me? No more than our good Doctor Karekezi!"

Cornelius decided to take the bull by its horns:

"If we must fight, let's do it with our faces uncovered, Skipper. My father committed this abominable crime, yes, but I'm not going to let myself be destroyed because of him."

Cornelius's resoluteness seemed to impress Gérard:

"I drank blood, so I did," he said less harshly, turning his head away.

That answer surprised Cornelius. At the Café des Grands Lacs he had already said almost the same thing and it had intrigued him. But it wasn't the moment to ask questions. Cornelius wanted to say something, but changed his mind when he heard Gérard crying softly.

ϡ

"You went there?" asked Siméon.

"Yes," Cornelius answered simply.

"Did you see everything?"

"Yes."

"Good."

The night was clear and mild. They spoke so softly that they seemed like two shadows in the middle of the courtyard. Siméon, self-possessed as always, was deep in thought.

"The bodies are intact," said Cornelius.

"Yes, they're the ones that were in the middle of the big graves at the Polytechnic. During the first days, you could recognize certain people. Some of the Murambi townspeople know which ones are their relatives among those remains. . . . They go there, look at the bodies, then leave. Did Gérard tell you that at first, blood came up to the surface?"

"No."

"Above each grave we saw little puddles of blood forming, Cornelius. At night, dogs came to quench their thirst."

A shiver ran through Cornelius's body. He had a fleeting image of a band of dogs drinking leisurely, by the light of the moon, the blood of the victims of Murambi. He imagined the reflection of the moon in the lake of blood.

The dogs: vague and somber forms, cut straight out of the darkness.

He thought that Siméon was looking for a way to open the world of symbols to him. In his quest for himself he was listening for cues from the old man. Thanks to him he would master the signs and know how to read the mysteries.

"Monsters drinking the blood of Rwanda. I understand the symbol, Siméon Habineza."

"It's not a symbol," said Siméon softly. "Our eyes saw it."

"Is it possible?"

"Our eyes saw it," repeated Siméon.

After a pause he added:

"No, there was no sign, Cornelius. Don't listen to those who claim to have seen spots of blood on the moon before the massacres. Nothing of the sort happened. The wind didn't howl with sorrow during the night, nor did the trees start to talk to each other about the folly of men. It was all very simple. Here in our region one of the prefects had said: 'No, none of these barbarous crimes here.' They immediately killed him. We knew that our turn would come. Then, one night, I went to look at the houses up there. It was a night like tonight, peaceful and clear, but there were fewer lights than usual on the Murambi hill. And then, yes, I reflected that every home without a light was a future tomb."

Cornelius was obsessed by the image of the lake of blood.

"How is that possible, Siméon?"

"That is how it is, and it is the work of your father. I wanted you to know everything before coming to Murambi. I told Jessica and Stanley, 'Talk to him.' You see, in this business, many killed out of greed, out of stupidity, out of fear of the authorities, or I don't know what. Your father, Joseph, he knew what he was doing. As a cold-blooded and resolute killer, he knew better than anyone how to put trickery at the service of hatred. What were his studies good for? In class he was always the best. Sometimes I sit on that mat for hours and hours and I say to myself: 'Joseph, who was so intelligent, was he also completely insane? Is it possible?' He succeeded in tricking everyone. Nobody suspected a thing. In Murambi, the dying called on him for help. They believed that Doctor Karekezi didn't know that his charges were being massacred."

Cornelius saw again furtively the image of his mother, Nathalie. Had she understood, at the last minute? What could possibly go on in the mind of a woman who discovers such abject duplicity when there's nothing left that she can do? The same haunting thoughts kept coming back, under Siméon's calm gaze.

"Your mother, Nathalie, brought you into this world running, to escape from the people who wanted to kill her." Nathalie Kayumba. He would never know anything else about her. And her husband, his father, a young rural doctor with a feverish look, idealistic and reckless. It was enough for him to get involved with killers to make a good career for himself. But in those days, Joseph Karekezi had only scorn for such calculations.

"When did my father change?"

Siméon didn't respond immediately, content to look straight in front of him. Then he said:

"I'm going to tell you something else, Cornelius: even during the best years, Joseph couldn't stand to see his enemies much wealthier than him. He looked down on them, knowing that in their eyes he was nothing, just a poor devil with impressive diplomas. He suffered a lot because of that. I saw it very clearly. When your father decided to become a powerful man, he knew that he would have blood on his hands. Since President Kayibanda's time, people were always killing Tutsis and then going home to play with their children. Tens dead. Hundreds dead. Thousands dead. They couldn't be bothered to count any more. Little by little it became routine. And your father must have said to himself: 'I'm an important doctor, I'm not going to die like a poor bastard.' Joseph Karekezi was never scared of anything or anyone. Besides, that's what it's like in our family, we're foolhardy. When a man like that decides to do evil, he is more dangerous than all the others."

"Siméon," said Cornelius suddenly, "didn't you at least have an inkling, you who knew him so well?"

Siméon slowly nodded his head:

"Yes, when I saw him gather all those people together in the school I sent for him and asked him: 'Joseph, you wouldn't be mixed up in this business, would you?' He seemed shocked: 'Me, Siméon?' 'Yes, you,' I answered calmly. Then he stared at me for a long time and asked: 'You're suspicious of me?' 'Yes,' I answered. He said that I had always been perceptive, but that my reasoning was starting to go askew. He reminded me that he hadn't been involved in politics for a long time. 'Too many things are happening now,' I told him, 'that only a month ago no one could ever have imagined, too many people around me have gone mad.' He settled comfortably into his chair, intertwined his fingers as he often did and said, leaning toward me: 'All of this is nothing but a *muyaga*, Siméon. . . . ' Do you know what a *muyaga* is, Cornelius?"

"It's an ill wind, a difficult but fleeting period."

"Correct. Then your father said: 'We've already had

them, periods like this, it'll pass.' Then he swore to me on
his faith as a Christian that he had absolutely no bad intentions, before adding: 'I'm between two bloods, Siméon,
if I start killing, what will I do with Nathalie and the
children?' I pointed out to him, 'There's only one blood,
Joseph, have you forgotten that?' It was only later that I
realized that he had let the phrase slip. But he didn't get
flustered. 'Very well,' he said with a laugh, 'you know as
well as I do that it's just a way of speaking. Besides, to
prove my good faith, I'm going to take Nathalie and the
children to the school.' He loved your mother and he was
literally crazy about his two kids. That reassured me. Only
I didn't know quite how determined they were this time
round. And I quickly discovered something strange: your
father had a cold and empty heart, he neither loved nor
hated anyone and that's why he was able to kill so many
innocent people at once."

Then Siméon told him the story of the farewell ceremony.

Doctor Joseph Karekezi had come back to see him with
Nathalie and the two children, dressed up like a little
prince and princess. Rich kids, boisterous and lively, but
so fragile too.

"Julienne and François always called me grandfather,
although I was only their uncle. I always looked so much
older than Joseph. They told me that they would have
their own room to play in at the Polytechnic. Your mother
was silent, as usual. She gazed lovingly at them with
a tender look. She seemed to be a happy and peaceful
woman. Joseph was her god. He had completely effaced
her and she saw the world only through her husband's
eyes. At a certain point your name came up and Joseph
said that he had talked with you by phone the night before."

"It's true," said Cornelius, scornfully.

But he was immediately tempted to smile as he had on the day that Jessica had told him the story for the first time.

"Only one person saw it all clearly," continued Siméon.

Cornelius gave a start:

"Who's that?"

"Gérard Nayinzira. The one who wanted to be a sailor. He guessed your father's intentions just in time. He owes his life to that."

ટ☙

It was his first outing in Murambi. From the intersection that took the place of a real business center, a long avenue divided the city from west to east. Murambi was soulless and dead. The feeling of languor was heightened by the old-fashioned offices and businesses that lined the main avenue here and there. On a hotel patio he saw ten or so customers seated at tables with bottles of beer and cups of coffee in front of them. Some of them, slumped in their chairs, looked around them morosely. Foreigners on assignment, no doubt, required to stay in Murambi for a few days, but who would much rather have been somewhere else. As in Kigali, white or yellow Japanese minibuses went through the streets in search of passengers on their way to nearby places. He had gotten off one of those very minibuses the day he arrived. The few pedestrians were stony-faced. Some of them turned around when he passed by, out of curiosity or perhaps to help him find his way. It was easy to guess by his halting manner that he didn't know the town very well.

He went into a spare parts shop to find out where the house that Doctor Joseph Karekezi had lived in before he fled to Zaïre was. The shopkeeper was dozing behind the counter. A faint smile lit his face when the stranger introduced himself as Siméon Habineza's nephew.

"I know Siméon well," said the man, extracting himself from his niche to come toward him.

"My name is Cornelius Uvimana and I'm the son of Joseph Karekezi, the doctor."

"So you're the one who was abroad?"

"Yes," answered Cornelius.

He thought that the shopkeeper was going to add something, but he merely gave him the information he had asked for. However, between sentences his eyes were riveted on him.

Cornelius thanked him and set off. Almost immediately, by a parking lot, he stopped, took out some bills from his jacket pocket and counted them. "There's enough to call Djibouti," he told himself. He wanted to talk to Zakya. He turned back. The salesman, who hadn't moved from his spot, had watched him leave with curiosity. Cornelius spoke to him again:

"I'd like to go to the post office first. Is it far from here?"

The man, slightly annoyed, pointed out the offices fifty yards behind them.

"You see that black car that the kid is washing?"

"Yes."

"It's parked right in front of the post office."

Zakya wasn't there. He got her brother Idriss on the line and promised to call back later. In any case, the line was bad. He resigned himself to sending a postcard that he bought at one of the booths.

When he passed by the spare parts shop again, the salesman was at the entrance to his shop with two men and a young woman. He had obviously informed them that

Doctor Karekezi's son was around. They spoke softly as they watched him.

Cornelius crossed a lot of some sort. Across the way he saw chauffeurs in uniform standing next to big cars and gardeners busy trimming flowering hedges. Murambi's residential neighborhood looked like any other residential neighborhood. Silence. Boredom. Drowsy happiness. Without any trouble he recognized the long white wall the man had told him to look for. Even from afar, one sensed that Doctor Joseph Karekezi's house had been abandoned for a long time.

Gérard Nayinzira was waiting for him in front of the gate.

He read the inscription in white letters on a blue plaque, covered with dust, "The House of Happiness." Inside, everything evoked the insistent vulgar display of the nouveau riche. A swimming pool in the form of a giant fish. A tennis court surrounded by high railings. Trees with white and purple flowers, crowded together along a path of triangular flagstones. The estate was so large that the apartments—a pink and white three story edifice— seemed very far in front of him. "This is Africa," he thought bitterly, "all these people who want to live in houses bigger than a school. Our problem isn't our poverty, but our rich people." He ranted on to himself: "Besides, it's easy, they gather people together in schools to massacre them!"

Gérard, who up to then had made sure to keep a good distance from him, went ahead of him onto the veranda. In the foyer that looked like a waiting room, the same fine layer of dust had settled on the padded armchairs and the wooden sculptures.

The badly lit hallway leading to the staircase smelled

musty. But everything was intact, and every object was in its place.

An old dog, its black hair now grizzled, raised its curled tail and wandered up to them lethargically.

"This must be the famous Taasu. The children talked about him all the time on the phone. They adored him."

"The doctor also loved his dog very much."

Cornelius noticed Gérard's sour tone, that he thought was intended to hurt him. "He's going to hold it against me still for a long time," he said to himself. He pretended not to have noticed anything.

"Why didn't he take Taasu with him?"

"Colonel Perrin refused," answered Gérard. "I was up there," he added, raising his head toward the trees. "I saw them. In the end, they hated each other, he and the colonel."

"It's like a play," said Cornelius, dreaming. "How did it happen?"

"It was very early in the morning. The colonel said, 'No, not the dog.' The doctor protested, 'I'm not leaving without Taasu.' Then the colonel said dryly: 'You're joking? You liquidate thousands of people, you kill your wife and your children, and you get all worked up about this animal! I don't have time for this. Goodbye.' He left him there and went back to his car. I saw the doctor hesitate, then stroke Taasu one last time before running to join the colonel, a suitcase in each hand. It was grotesque. Doctor Karekezi. A man who used to be so proud. He got to the car all sweaty and out of breath. The colonel looked at him scornfully and said, 'You're breathless, Doctor.' I had a desire to come out of my hiding place and shout at him: 'Here I am, Doctor Karekezi, I was in the Polytechnic and I'm not dead, no one can kill the whole world!'"

There was an almost unbearable violence in Gérard's words and gestures. He added that the doctor had begged Colonel Perrin to let him take some of his little possessions with him.

"The colonel authorized him to do so?"

"Of course," said Gérard, "he was intent on humiliating him through and through."

"He was defeated," said Cornelius, surprised at his own jubilation.

"A total collapse. That will always be the best day of my life."

Gérard's voice was also hard, tense, and vibrant with a hateful joy.

"You know, Skipper, I know your story."

A shadow came over Gérard's face:

"You mean the way I was able to escape the carnage?"

Cornelius sensed that Gérard was hiding something. He too had a heavy secret to bear.

"No. I just learned that you had guessed my father's intentions."

Gérard seemed relieved.

"Ah! He came to visit us on the eve of the massacre. Before arriving at the school I had seen some absolutely unbearable things. I could no longer believe in the goodness of men. I often thought to myself when I looked at the soldiers who were assigned to take care of us: 'We're screwed.' But I had no way of knowing what was in store for us. So when your father appeared, I went up to him. I insulted him in front of everyone, just to see. He wasn't used to it. He was a god there. While he was trying to reassure me, our eyes met, and at that instant I understood everything. I understood that we were all going to die."

Gérard stopped, then said in a low voice:

"I found a way, I wanted to save my own skin. . . . I couldn't do anything for the others."

Cornelius was surprised to hear himself talking like Siméon:

"In this whole affair, everyone has his secrets. Keep yours for yourself, Skipper."

Gérard told him that he had gone to find Siméon after the massacre. Siméon had advised him to take refuge at Doctor Karekezi's, the only safe place in Murambi.

"I got myself into the branches of a tree, in the rear courtyard, and waited for him."

Taasu, who was bored with them, waddled off around the courtyard.

"Don't be offended, Gérard," said Cornelius, starting to climb the stairs, "but I want to be alone when I visit the bedrooms."

"That's impossible," said Gérard, moving forward. "I'm coming with you."

"Why?" asked Cornelius, surprised.

"Siméon. He insisted."

"What is in those rooms?"

"Nothing. They've been empty and abandoned for four years. The old man insisted. I don't know why."

They went all through the other floors, which consisted of at least thirty rooms, some of which were huge. Cornelius sat down on one of the twins' beds in the children's room. School notebooks lay on the floor among colorful toys. He read the initials on a notebook: J.K. How old had he been when he asked his father the question that had been bothering him for so long? While he was accompanying him to the house of one of his patients, he had suddenly asked him:

"What's behind the hills, Papa?"

His father had immediately snapped: "Nothing."

In the end, this was the only memory of him that he had. One word. The word "nothing." It might as well be nothing. His father must have said it without thinking. But what did it matter to him from now on? In his eyes, Doctor Karekezi, no doubt wandering around somewhere between Goma and Bukavu, was neither dead nor alive. How could he have gone back on his word to that extent? Just to get rich? An appetite for power, that glaring mask of infamy and servitude.

Documents were lying on the velvet carpet in Doctor Karekezi's office, including some photo albums that he didn't have the heart to open. He put them on a small table and then picked them back up again. He had seen the remains in Murambi. He should look at these photos too. This house was a graveyard. In the snapshots you could see how the doctor had thickened out over the years. The young man with the resolute and even slightly violent look, in spite of his dreamy eyes and his intellectual's glasses, had, toward the end, acquired the typical appearance of a prominent person, slightly balding, with a lackluster, worried look about him.

Turning the pages of the album, Cornelius felt Gérard's attentive eyes on him. He had to overcome his hesitation to ask him:

"What did my father do on the night of the massacre?"

"There was a meeting with Colonel Musoni and some important people who had come from Kigali and elsewhere. The doctor gave orders. Everyone obeyed him."

"I'm going to take quite a few things away with me from here," said Cornelius.

"The police beat you to it. They've been here several times."

"That's understandable," said Cornelius simply.

Cornelius organized several documents in a file. There were addresses and telephone numbers—including his in Djibouti—as well as a notebook in which the doctor wrote down his appointments and quickly scribbled down his impressions. He also took some of his mother's things. All these would help him, even if he didn't know how yet, to do up the loose and frayed threads of his existence. He knew: accepting his past was the price he had to pay to begin to recover his serenity and sense of the future.

"I find it strange that the townspeople of Murambi haven't taken possession of the place," he observed.

"They tried. They wanted to break everything. Siméon spoke to them: 'When I was young, that's how things started. After destroying this house, you'll go back home. On the way some of you will say: a Hutu lives here, let's take his things and kill his children out of revenge. But afterwards, you won't be able to stop for many years. I want to tell you this: you have suffered, but that doesn't make you any better than those who made you suffer. They are people like you and me. Evil is within each one of us. I, Siméon Habineza, repeat, that you are not better than them. Now, go back home and think about it: there comes a time when you have to stop shedding blood in a country. Each one of you must have the strength to believe that that moment is here. If someone among you is not strong enough, then he's no better than an animal. My brother's house will not be destroyed. It will be a home for all the orphans who hang about on the streets of Murambi. And I'm going to say one last thing to you: let not one of you try, when the moment comes, to find out if those orphans are Twa, Hutu, or Tutsi.' No one dared insist. In Murambi, everyone knows who Siméon Habineza is."

"He's a free man," said Cornelius. "You must know the

proverb: 'The man who has no fence around his house is a man who has no enemies.' Siméon has no fence around his mind."

"Yes, but be careful, Cornelius: these days Siméon detests proverbs and everything else that they call ancient wisdom," remarked Gérard.

"He's changed a lot."

"Can I give you my opinion?"

"Of course," said Cornelius.

"Even with regard to religion, he is more or less indifferent now, the old man. He thinks that our people were betrayed by Imana."

"Did he tell you that?"

"No."

Cornelius remembered Siméon's words from a few days earlier: "No, there was no sign, Cornelius. . . . " Did he think that a pact had been broken?

Every day at dawn Cornelius was roused from sleep by the soft dry tapping of Siméon's walking stick on the steps. He listened to the noise wane slowly, then turned over to face the wall, his mind still foggy. The ritual, familiar and reassuring, announced Siméon's walk through Murambi. But that morning he couldn't go back to sleep. In the middle of the night he had gotten up to take a Detensor pill. The only effect the sleeping pill had had was to increase his agitation. Eyes open in the dark, he tried unsuccessfully to put some order in his ideas. Memories, whether distant or recent, jostled about in his mind, refusing to leave him alone. They passed each other, brushed against each other and sometimes collided with each other before slowly dissipating. From this chaos there emerged some feelings and images that were clear enough: Zakya, whom he had not been able to get in touch with for several days; the death mask—or clown's face—among the remains in Murambi; the mixture of hostility and sympathy that he felt from the inhabitants of the little town; Gérard's tenacious and silent rancor; Stanley and Jessica. They were supposed to arrive in Murambi that morning. Just thinking about it made him ill at ease. He was almost ashamed to see them again. It was his father's fault. He had betrayed their childhood.

He had a sudden urge to sit on the stone bench in front of the house to watch Siméon turn the corner of the street.

Black hat on his head and a scarf pulled tightly around his neck to protect him from the dew, Siméon walked leaning on his cane, his step slow and regular. Cornelius felt overcome with a sudden sadness at the premonition he had before his eyes at that exact moment: the very image of Siméon's death.

It was unthinkable that so much splendor—it reminded him of the child playing the flute near Lake Mohazi—had nothing to do with the impending death of the old man. An indescribable power emanated from him. Little did it matter how many more years Siméon would live. Cornelius would always see him filling the deserted street with his presence. Thus, in the very country where death had worked away at destroying all energy, the force of life remained intact.

Back from his walk, Siméon came to join him on the stone bench.

Despite the energy he had just expended, his face was composed and his eyes shone with a beautiful light.

"You got up early this morning, Cornelius. What's going on?"

"I wanted to be there for your walk, that's all."

Siméon shrugged, amused:

"You could have come with me. I went into Joseph's house. The young people have already put in the mattresses for the orphans. Jessica will come from Kigali every once in a while to help them."

"Gérard too. He's very happy to be able to lend a hand."

"You won't be able to. I know."

"Later. I need time."

"It's time to talk to Siméon," thought Cornelius.

"For the moment, I want to ask forgiveness for what my father did."

Siméon remained impassive. Cornelius had the feeling that he had caught him by surprise.

"Do you want to go back to the Polytechnic?"

Cornelius hesitated:

"Maybe. I don't know."

"Everyone has to look for his truth alone. No one will be able to help you."

"Not even you?"

"You must be like the solitary traveler, Cornelius. If he gets lost, he looks up at the sky and the trees, he looks all around him. But the traveler could have said to himself, bending down toward the ground: 'I'm going to ask the path, who has been here for such a long time, he'll surely be able to help me.' Now, the path will never show him the way to go. The path does not know the way."

"I can't find words to speak to the dead."

He detected a fleeting expression of annoyance—or maybe of anger—on the old man's face.

"There are no words to speak to the dead," said Siméon in a tense voice. "They won't get up to answer you. What you'll learn there is that everything is quite over for the dead of Murambi. And maybe then you'll respect human life more. Our lives are brief, they are like strings of illusions that die, like little bubbles in our entrails. We don't even know what game it's playing at with us, but we have nothing else. It's the only thing that's more or less certain on this earth."

For the first time since his return to Rwanda Cornelius felt tears welling up under his eyelids.

It was an unforgettable morning. While the neighborhood was waking up little by little, they stayed seated on the stone bench for hours. Siméon spoke to him for a long time. It was, without doubt, the end of something. Siméon had waited for him. He had come, and now, they were saying their goodbyes.

"Four years ago people said: 'Times are difficult, maybe if we kill one part of the population everything will get better.' Wasn't that an incredible way of thinking? Young girls killed their fathers. Mothers killed their sons. Husbands killed their wives. And they all did it joyfully. They got together in churches to make raucous fun of dying human beings."

He continued, saying that he, Siméon, could not understand the crowd's joy, which to him seemed much more difficult to bear than the moans of the dying. Each time he thought of it, he felt ashamed of being Rwandan.

Then Siméon spoke to him of his childhood.

In his early years he was told about the arrival of the first European. Some people still remembered it. He was a German. He had asked to be received by the Mwami in the royal court of Nyanza. His stranger's eyes couldn't keep still in his affable and smiling face. You would think that he thought and listened with his eyes. He stared for a long time at all kinds of things, as if to pierce them simply by his gaze. Without saying a word about himself, he asked questions. They hastened to answer them. Before coming to Rwanda he had subdued, on the coast and far away in the interior of the land, people who were similar to those of Rwanda. Nobody knew that. Coming from far away, he had brought gifts that no one had ever seen.

They celebrated him.

Then came the missionaries. At first the padres kept quiet. They spent their days in the bush. What were they doing there? Some said they had seen them examining plants and rocks or stretching ropes above hills to take measurements. Was it true or false? No one knew. At nightfall, they closed themselves inside a hut to sing by the glow of candles. Then they started to convert their domestic servants. Soon they asked the Mwami to get rid of the drum of Kalinga. "We're going to play the drum," they said, "and nothing will happen to us." They did, and nothing happened to them. Then they said to the Mwami: "If you continue to worship objects, your soul will be damned, you will burn in the flames of hell and you will suffer immeasurable pain." They demanded that Imana's name be changed. Our men, full of good sense, replied that that was folly. The padres punished them mercilessly. They forced them to swallow sacred cowries mixed with jam. Siméon Habineza's own father was one of those who dared to revolt. Yes, his father had refused. One of the padres hit him violently on the chest. His father got up and said to him, "What a bad god is yours, white man, that you can make me worship him only by force and not by persuasion!" The Mwami himself warned his subjects, "A terrible tragedy will befall us because of this new god. I am telling you. Do not change the name of Imana, the world belongs to those who give a name to God." But all was already lost. Many chiefs had converted to the new religion. The foreigners got rid of the recalcitrant Mwami and put another in his place. For the first time in their life the people of Rwanda saw a Mwami wear a helmet, boots, a jacket, and trousers. He was a very vain young man who took to strutting through the streets of the royal city of Nyanza to have people admire his fancy clothes. When the padres gave him a car, he almost went crazy. For everyone, the Mwami was the very presence of God on earth. To see their god going to mass on Sunday was a terrible shock for those who did not want to change Imana's name under any circumstances. The world was no longer recognizable. Every day that passed was different from the others. The padres had won.

Siméon spoke again of the massacres organized after the death of President Habyarimana. Who was responsible for those barbarous acts? He had heard accusations against foreigners. Some said that it was all their fault. Maybe it was true. But Siméon himself still wanted an explanation for the rejoicing of the crowds in Kibungo, in Mugonero, or in Murambi. He thought he knew the history of Rwanda, but he couldn't see anything there that could justify such a vicious hatred. In the past, the foreigners had said to the Tutsis, "You are superb, your noses are long and your skin is light, you are tall and your lips are thin, you cannot be blacks, a twist of fate led you to be among these savages. You come from somewhere else." What should we be more amazed at? The audacity of the foreigners or the incredible stupidity of people back then? But, added Siméon, there was no point in moaning, lying on the ground. For all that, the conquerors won't regret having been the strongest. They won't say, "I'm sorry to have conquered your country, it was a mistake, I'm really very sorry." They won't even think that they've committed a crime. No, those who fought to subdue a nation through trickery or cruelty have nothing to be forgiven about. They won't be ashamed of their success. That has never happened in the history of mankind.

Siméon said:

"I know the damage that foreigners did to us, four years ago and well before. But that damage was only possible because we were not free people. Have we ever been bothered by our chains? Sometimes I think not. We can't hold our own lack of pride against anybody else."

Siméon said again, forcefully:

"Cornelius Uvimana?"

"Yes."

"Do you hear me?"

"I hear you, Siméon Habineza."

"Finally, there is only one name for what happened four years ago: defeat. Since the time of the Mwamis, puppets have been named head of the country by unknown people. That has to stop. So, Cornelius, if the master is a slave, we shouldn't obey him. We have to fight him. I'd like you to remember that, come what may."

"The way I should remember the child with the flute on the shores of Lake Mohazi," said Cornelius. "I know it's the same."

"You've understood me."

"That's at least one symbol, isn't it, Siméon Habineza?"

"You know that I don't like those words that have so often masked our servitude, but maybe that child is in fact one."

Siméon's words were very pure. In the autumn of his life he still dared to behave like the solitary traveler. In the end, what he was saying was simply this: all the spilled blood should make people pull themselves together.

Siméon picked up his walking stick.

"I'm going to my room. The sunlight hurts my eyes a bit."

Cornelius hesitated, then said:

"I'm sad to hear you speak like that."

"I can guess why. Don't worry, I don't feel my hour approaching. I had the opportunity to speak to you this morning and I did it. That's all."

"I understand," said Cornelius.

But he didn't altogether think so.

His two friends arrived around noon.

No sooner had she settled herself on the mat than Jessica started to tease Siméon.

"I'm still waiting for my love poem, old Siméon."

"Child, I played in the court of the Mwami," said Siméon. "We had poetry contests for our beloved."

Jessica pretended to be angry:

"You dare talk to me about girls that you've loved?"

She was the only one who wasn't intimidated by Siméon. They held a profound admiration for each other. Siméon never spoke about the trials of his life. But the previous evening he had said to Cornelius, "Jonas Sibomana's daughter makes me forget all the children I've lost." In her he saw the kind of person that Rwanda needed in order to come to terms with itself.

Stanley was quiet. Cornelius noticed that he was watching him attentively, just as he had the day when he had come with Jessica to welcome him at the airport. Cornelius thought that in the end, of the two of them, it was Stan who suffered the most.

*

A bird swooped in among the trees and its brief cry was immediately lost in the night. In the distance, a pack of dogs barked at a passing automobile. For a moment, the headlights lit up a corner of the horizon toward the north, then everything became dark again.

A bit further down, the town was sleeping. But Cornelius knew from experience that it was the most difficult time of day for the Murambi townspeople, the moment when bitter memories resurfaced. Perhaps they had seen, early in the morning at a street corner, the man who four years earlier had slit the throats of all their family members. But it didn't even have to be that. A mere suggestion was enough to bring the torment back to life: the color or cut of a dress, a melody, or the sound of a voice.

Sitting right on the ground, his eyes half closed and his mind empty, brought him a strong feeling of inner peace. Even though he knew nothing of the world of dreams, he felt as if he had been plunged into it, wide awake, for several hours. Everything conspired to make the moment unreal: trees slowly raising their fine black trunks toward the sky and the indistinct traces of footsteps on the red sand.

He felt his solitude like the muffled echo of that of the victims. Well before the Interahamwe arrived, everyone was already alone, torn between anguish and absurd hopes.

Gérard Nayinzira had finally decided to tell him about how he had managed to escape the Murambi massacre. "I had come from Bisesero. Over there, we had all withdrawn to Muyira Hill. We had told Aminadabu Birara, 'Everyone respects you, you will be our chief.' The weaker ones went to gather stones and we used them to defend ourselves as best we could. Despite the rain, the cold, and the privation, we formed a compact bloc. Aminadabu Birara stood behind us to show us how to man our positions. When he gave the order, we tore down the hillside en masse to charge the Interahamwe, to force them into hand-to-hand combat and cause some losses among them. We were even able to get two or three of their guns. If we were able to hold out for a long time, it was only because they were never able to disperse us. So I knew that in

Murambi your father's soldiers would come first, armed with grenades and automatic weapons. In the panic, those who became separated would be cut into pieces by the Interahamwe. I decided that in order to save my skin I would stick with a group, come what may. Even when the soldiers started to shoot bursts in every direction, my mind stayed very clear. I allowed myself to be covered by the bodies of the first victims. But I was still half visible. So I prayed really hard for others to fall next to me and that's what happened. I had blood on my clothes, in my eyes, everywhere." At that moment in Gérard's account, he and Cornelius looked at each other in silence. Cornelius said softly, "You had it in your mouth too, Skipper?" "What do you mean?" "In the Café des Grands Lacs you said, 'My blood is full of blood.' You don't realize it, but you talk about it all the time." Then Gérard lowered his voice, "Yes, I was obliged to swallow and then spit out their blood, it went into my whole body. During those minutes I thought that maybe trying to survive wasn't the right decision. I was tempted a thousand times to let myself die. Something was calling me, something with a terrible power: it was nothingness. A sort of dizziness. I had the feeling that there would be something like happiness to throw into the emptiness. But I kept splashing around in their blood. You know, blood's nothing, poets have ended up making it seem almost beautiful. Shed your blood for your Country. The blood of Martyrs. You're telling me. It doesn't mean anything, Cornelius, urine and excrement spread all over the ground, old women running naked, the noise of limbs shattering, and all these hallucinating looks, strapping fellows who use the wounded as shields against the machetes, that doesn't tell you anything about all those unfortunates who despise each other so much that they don't even dream of hating their torturers: on the contrary, I heard them begging. The Interahamwe were dressed in rags, they stank of bad beer, but they were gods, because they had the power to kill, no one could stop them, and you should have seen their victims with their emaciated faces open their arms to them in a gesture of desperate love! In Bisesero things were different. By resisting the killers we forced them to remain beings of flesh and blood like ourselves. They were scared of dying, they were so delicate. Even the idea of getting a few scratches was intolerable, that wasn't part of the plan, their plan had been to slit the throats of a few innocent people, to go off and have a good time, to take themselves away somewhere else to torture some more innocent people and so on. We made them feel that it wasn't as easy as all that. On that Muyira Hill, each one of us could see in the other's face how proud we were to fight, to refuse to allow ourselves to be taken docilely to the slaughterhouse like livestock. Oh yes, I saw the difference. And all the beautiful words of the poets, Cornelius, can say nothing, I swear to you, of the fifty thousand ways to die like a dog, within a few hours. In Murambi, at the beginning of the attack, I saw an Interahamwe rape a young woman under a tree. His boss came by and shouted at him: 'Hey, Simba, everywhere we go it's always the same story, first the women, the women, the women! Hurry up and finish your push-ups, we promised Papa we'd do a good job!' The boss took a couple of steps, then, changing his mind, came back to crush the young woman's head with a big stone, and in a single blow there was just this red and white pulp in place of the skull. That didn't stop the Interahamwe who kept working away at the twitching body. His eyes were popping out of his head, raised upwards, I think he was even more excited than before." Gérard had insisted, "I saw that with my own eyes. Do you believe me, Cornelius? It's important that you believe me. I'm not making it up, for once that's not necessary. If you prefer to think that I imagined these horrors your mind will be at peace and that's not good. This pain will get lost in opaque words and everything will be forgotten until the next massacre. They really did all these incredible things. It happened in Rwanda only four years ago, when the entire world was playing soccer in America. Sometimes I go back to Murambi. I look at the place where my remains would have been and I tell myself that something's wrong, I move my hands and my feet because it seems strange to me that they're still there, and my entire body seems like a hallucination to me." After another longer pause Gérard had said, for maybe the tenth time, "I couldn't do anything for them. I didn't have much time to think. It would have been useless to resist, it wasn't like in Bisesero, in Murambi they had been camping for days up on top of the hill."

Cornelius was well aware that the genocide was not one of those action films where the weak could always count on the last-minute arrival of a strong and brave young hero. Rather than dreaming of reproaching him, he admired Gérard's courage. He had needed it to be able to get to his confession. Cornelius just hoped that this secret he had shared with him would be Gérard Nayinzira's first step toward forgiveness.

Loneliness was also the young woman in black who came almost every day to the Polytechnic. She knew exactly which of all the tangled skeletons lying on the cold concrete were those of her little girl and her husband. She would go straight to one of the sixty-four doors of Murambi and stand in the middle of the room before two intertwined corpses: a man clutching a decapitated child against him. The young woman in black prayed in silence, and then left.

The Polytechnic was a crossroads, one of the few places in Rwanda where all actors in the tragedy had met: victims, torturers, and foreign troops with Operation Turquoise. The latter had set up camp, in full knowledge, on top of the mass graves. That was extremely bad manners. Had they believed, then, by behaving in such a way, that Murambi's dead were somehow missing that little something that made them human beings? Had they believed that they were missing a soul, or something of the sort?

Cornelius thought of the Old Man.

"In those countries a genocide doesn't mean much."

Probably not even a detail. The Old Man. A bitter heart. A cold spirit. A curt voice. Offended, they said, to discover all too late that he was, after all, mortal. A bouquet of flowers for the Widow. Scornful words for the victims. History would bring him down a peg or two. But in the end it didn't matter very much. Cornelius felt only the slightest bitterness. He was confident of the future, of its long memory and infinite patience. Sooner or later, in Africa and elsewhere, people will say calmly, "Let's talk about the hundred days in Rwanda again, there is no unimportant genocide, Rwanda, *neither,* is not just a minor detail of contemporary history."

Cornelius was much more troubled by the calls to reason coming from those he admired or with whom he shared a close friendship. These foreigners, as horrified as he was by the killing at Kigarama, Nyamata, and elsewhere, had understood this: a genocide reminds every society of its essential fragility. But they invited him to step back: "Yes, it's all terrible," they said, "but there is

life after the genocide, it's time to move on." A long list of
the world's abominations almost always followed. He saw
again, as if hallucinating, a thousand terrible scenes. Freetown. Streets where corpselike children wandered, their
eyes bright and wild. It wasn't enough to kill anymore.
They have to go for the soul too. Enter the rebels who
know only too well how to create human suffering. Let's
try, they say, the eternal agony of a people without arms
or legs. And they went to work.

He did his best to explain: almost a million dead in such
a short space of time, it was truly unique in the history of
humankind. They retorted—and he sensed a mixture of
pity and irony in his friends' gazes—Yes, but it's not a
game of numbers, each instance of suffering is as good as
millions of others. Why did he persist in taking all the
credit? It was sad to say, but he had to admit it: Rwanda
was not worth troubling the sleep of the universe about.
If he kept on speaking like this, they would suspect him
of bragging. . . .

What could he reply to that?

Strange times.

He felt torn apart.

The fourth genocide of the century remained an enigma
and perhaps the key could only be found in the head of a
madman or in the mysterious movement of planets. That
orgy of hatred went far beyond the struggle for power in
a little country. He dreamed of a God who had suddenly
become demented, parting the clouds and stars with angry, sweeping gestures, to descend onto Rwanda's soil.

That very afternoon—they were all there: Jessica, Stanley,
Gérard, and him—he had heard Siméon address Imana.
Siméon's song resonated in his head. The old man mur-
mured, accompanying himself on a zither:

"Ah! Imana, you astonish me, tell me what has made you so
angry, Imana! You let all this blood pour out
    on the hills where you used to come to rest at night. Where
do you spend your nights
      now? Ah! Imana, you amaze me! Tell me then
what I have done to you, I do not understand your anger!"

Yes, the matter was a decidedly obscure one.
Those cruel days were like nothing that had ever been
seen. Woven from flashes, they were threaded with all
manner of frenzy. Cornelius was conscious of it, he would
never be able to tame this whirlwind, its bright colors, its
howls and its furious twisting. At the very most, Siméon
had given him a presentiment: a genocide is not just any
kind of story, with a beginning and an end between which
more or less ordinary events take place. Without ever having written a line in his life, Siméon Habineza was, in his
own way, a real novelist, that is to say, when all is said
and done, a storyteller of the eternal.

Cornelius was slightly ashamed of having entertained
the idea of a play. But he wasn't giving up his enthusiasm
for words, dictated by despair, helplessness before the
sheer immensity of evil, and no doubt a nagging con-
science. He did not intend to resign himself to the definitive victory of the murderers through silence. Not being able to claim to rival Siméon Habineza in his ability
to evoke things, he reserved for himself a more modest
role. He would tirelessly recount the horror. With machete words, club words, words studded with nails, naked
words and—despite Gérard—words covered with blood
and shit. That he could do, because he saw in the genocide of Rwandan Tutsis a great lesson in simplicity. Every
chronicler could at least learn—something essential to his
art—to call a monster by its name.

That was why he had chosen to be next to his dead. He wanted neither to pray nor to cry. He expected no miracle in front of the petrified remains of Murambi.

Not a single echo remained of the thousands of cries of terror that went up one morning toward the sky. God had heard them. The case was closed. It's just that eternity is so short, whatever they might say. The lake of blood had already dried up. For many months vultures had picked the corpses clean of their last shreds of putrid flesh. Then they flew away toward some other distant grave, of which there was no shortage in the world. It came to Cornelius's mind that every day the vultures would leave new and mysterious trails in the sky, en route to countries where so many other corpses were rotting in the sun.

A slight noise alerted him that someone had just opened the gate to the Polytechnic.

Footsteps were coming near.

He let himself be soothed by their slight crunching on the sand. Soon the sound started to wane before abruptly stopping.

At first he thought that the visitor had turned back. But he felt a stronger and stronger human presence nearby.

Someone was standing behind him and was watching him silently.

The visitor had no doubt stopped, hesitant to come forward, surprised to find an unknown person there so early in the morning.

Cornelius should have stood up and gone up to the visitor, or at least reassured him with a hand signal. He didn't do anything.

The noise again, the footsteps on the sand told him that the person had decided to continue walking.

The form passed near him.

He recognized the young woman in black.

She obviously didn't want to be seen.

Coming up to where Cornelius was, she turned unexpectedly toward the left. He had hardly the time to glimpse at her profile.

Seeing her set off toward the main building, he thought that the path that led her to her dead would not be lost in the labyrinths of history.

She herself, was she dead or alive? Cornelius would have liked to be able to ask that question to those who, under the pretext of drawing up the exact figures of the genocide, threw numbers around furiously. Let's not exaggerate, sir, after all, there were only eight hundred thousand dead in Rwanda. No, one million two hundred thousand. Many more. Somewhat fewer. He wanted to ask them where the young woman in black should go in their graphs. But it was easy to understand: after such an ordeal, there was a little bit of death in everyone. Maybe there was less life left in the veins of that unknown woman than among the remains of Murambi.

The young woman in black was, however, the shadow that the early morning had been watching for a long time.

Cornelius decided to wait for her.

He had to see her face, listen to her voice. She had no reason to hide, and it was his duty to get as close as he could to all suffering. He wanted to say to the woman in black—as he would later to Zakya's children—that the dead of Murambi, too, had dreams, and that their most ardent desire was for the resurrection of the living.

Afterword

Boubacar Boris Diop

La Mise Hôtel. That was the curious, and perhaps unique, name of the hotel where our group of authors set down our luggage a certain month of July 1998. For the government of Kigali that had headquartered us there, we were what one might call "cumbersome visitors." The fact was that after two years of negotiations, our hosts still were not sure what exactly had brought us to their country. Maïmouna Coulibaly and Nocky Djedanoum had of course explained to them that we had come as "African brothers" to listen to the victims of the massacres of 1994 and to try, through our books, to make their suffering known to the entire world. But that only partially moved them. As far as I could tell, Kigali had long reacted with a mixture of irritation and amusement at the idea that we were going to write novels about the genocide of the Tutsis in Rwanda. *Fest'Africa's* interlocutors, all political leaders in the Rwandan Patriotic Front, had only recently come out from the bush where they had spent years as freedom fighters, and especially mistrusted our choir of belated mourners. Why this sudden interest in their history from "francophone" writers, and on top of that through a project partially funded by a French foundation? I would not understand their perplexity until later. At the time, I could not know that Venuste Kayimahe, one of the Rwandan participants (with Jean-Marie Vianney Rurangwa) in the *Fest'Africa* project, abandoned to the killers by his French superiors and colleagues from the French Embassy and Cultural

Center, had escaped death only by a miracle. I also did not know that in June 1994 the soldiers of the French military Operation Turquoise had, for weeks on end and with full knowledge of the facts, played volleyball over the mass graves of Murambi, a fact that a billboard, still very much visible over the site, recalls. In short, I did not yet know that France had been, to conjure the title of an excellent book by Jacques Morel, "at the heart of the genocide of the Tutsis." I certainly was not the only one in this position, and today I realize that without the intervention of Rwandan friends from Paris—and in particular, the late journalist Théogène Karabayinga—the residency "Rwanda: Writing by Duty of Memory" would never have taken place.

Kigali is not a large city, and word quickly spread that foreign writers were lodging in the poor and densely populated neighborhood of Nyamirambo. During the two months of our stay, the restaurant-bar of *La Mise Hôtel* never emptied. Besides one old massive and taciturn Belgian fellow, accused of pedophilia and awaiting judgment—or extradition?—we were the only occupants of the ten cramped, slightly gloomy, and sparsely furnished hotel rooms. It was from there that we traveled all over Rwanda to discover the mass graves like those in Nyarubuye—on the Tanzanian border—in Kigarama, or in Nyamata, but it was also there that we came to encounter the characters of our future novels. . . . Intellectuals, artists, or simple citizens wanted to entrust their personal drama to whomever would be willing to recount it; they shared a few glasses of "maracuja" or banana beer with us until late into the night. And they often confessed to us that they understood nothing about what had happened to them, so that we sometimes suspected that they were, paradoxically, relying on us to penetrate the mystery of such a radical and consuming hatred.

We know that there are writers who like to believe they are haunted by their characters, and there are even some who would have us believe they lose sleep toying with the idea that their hero will escape from the pages of the novel at any moment and break their skull with the stroke of an axe while barking, on top of that, all sorts of obscenities. But this fascination with imaginary creatures only makes sense because it is, literally, a *figment of the imagination*. What about when, suddenly, a being in flesh and blood sits in front of you, biting vigorously into his goat skewer, and begs you with many gestures, silences, and veiled appeals to make him into a fictional being? The ambiguity of this unusual type of "commissioned text" is very quickly apprehended, because although your interlocutor wants to be fictionalized, he doesn't actually want you to transform him into anyone besides himself. ... For individuals like me who had always stood on the opposite shore of metamorphosis—happy like a child to become in turn a poacher, a counterfeiter, or a clandestine smuggler—there was reason to feel intimidated. What certain literary critics later called, with a smug smile, our "Rwandan expedition," thus began under the banner of a troubling uncertainty that obliged us all, in one way or another, to think about how we conceived of writing itself.

But in the Rwanda of 1998 and the aftermath of the genocide, we found it challenging to find creative inspiration. To find ourselves, four years after the genocide, engaged with a country devastated by the murderous madness of *Hutu Power*, to be immersed in horrifying stories, unimaginable to the normal human mind, to try to understand them, all of this very quickly distances you from God only knows what kinds of voluptuous and aesthetic torments. We all found a way to cope as best we could, and in my case my journalistic background was a tremendous help: for two months, I just asked questions and listened in silence, with infinite patience, to what people were willing to share. Besides, works and films on the history of Rwanda had been put at our disposal in one of the rooms of *La Mise Hôtel*, converted into a center of documentation, and I studied them carefully. It was essential in my eyes not only to accumulate the maximum amount of information on the genocide but also to find the key to the following enigma: in Kibungo, Butare, and elsewhere in Rwanda, in other words not that far, at least emotionally, from my native Senegal, some ten thousand people per day had been slaughtered without a single day of interruption for one hundred days, and four long

years after, I still knew virtually nothing about this bloody orgy.
. . . How can you consider yourself an intellectual able, in the
words of Cheikh Hamidou Kane, to "burn at the heart of things,"
if you do not even know to ask yourself why, overnight, so many
mutilated Tutsis corpses had been dropped in the Nyabarongo
or thrown to the dogs, and who was responsible? Why had I
not been able to see *just one* of these hundreds of thousands of
corpses? By inspiring me to ask such questions, the testimony of
survivors and my own readings relentlessly held me a mirror in
which my grave deficiencies were displayed. . . . Journalist and
writer, supposedly curious in world affairs since my early youth,
sympathetic to leftist ideas and an admirer of the Pan Africanism
of Cheikh Anta Diop, I had let myself be fooled, with a worrisome
ease, when it came to the mechanisms and political stakes of an
African catastrophe of cosmic dimensions. But who had fooled
me in this way? Convinced that it was CNN and company's fault,
a mischievous and irrefutable Wolof proverb came to my mind: *If*
someone lends you their eyes, don't be surprised, friend, if you're forced,
whatever you do, to see only what he wants you to see. . . . In today's
world, are the global media not ultimately the universal "lenders
of eyes?" We are all condemned to believe what their cameras tell
us, and the worst is that often the babbling tide of their images and
commentaries hides reality to a greater degree than their silences
or omissions. But even though they acted like they only saw in
the genocide of the Tutsis in Rwanda a mass crime of gigantic
proportions, picturesque and without rhyme or reason—in the
end, just one more "African thing"—no one has the right to hold
them accountable for their own blindness.

The problem for us Africans is perhaps above all our insensitiv-
ity, something that deserves further attention.

I will do so by evoking my own experience.

Since the publication of *Murambi, The Book of Bones* in 2000, I
have had the opportunity of discussing its content with the most
diverse of audiences around the world. It brings me no pleasure
in saying this, but I nevertheless have to admit that it is in Africa
itself that I still encounter the greatest reluctance to show an

interest in the One Hundred Days of Slaughter in Rwanda, and where the refusal to analyze the specific mechanisms that were in place, or for that matter to simply discuss them, is the most apparent. It is also, it seems to me, on this continent that information about the Rwandan tragedy remains the most lacking. Are we to attribute such a shocking indifference to this "habit of unhappiness" that brings to mind the title of one of Mongo Beti's novel? It's certainly true that the struggle for power in Liberia, Sierra Leone, the Democratic Republic of Congo, and in a number of other places over the course of the past decades has been characterized by such a succession of horrors that we may very well have become immunized to the worst atrocities. Indeed, there have been so many massacres that one can find oneself thinking that none of them actually occurred. It's a paradox but maybe only in appearance: so many scenes of cruelty in the heart of the forest, mutually abolishing one another, end up etched into our imaginations like a harmless, even natural, nuisance. This, however, does not mean that we adapt to it: every African has borne the burden of the bloody crimes of Mobutu or Idi Amin Dada and suffered their antics like a personal humiliation. This all ends up weighing heavily on our minds and the resulting amnesia, more deliberate than may at first appear, is more likely than not an individual survival strategy than the result of indifference.

This very understandable discomfort does not justify the strange little disdainful pout with which some people let slip, at the first opportunity, that Rwanda may very well be important, yes, but "all the same, let's not go overboard." . . . To my knowledge, African intellectuals are the only ones to refuse, under the most diverse and varied, but often highly eccentric pretexts, to take into account historical facts that can have such serious consequences on the fate of future generations. To listen to them speak or to read their chic and complacent texts, you soon realize that a form of "right-thinking" is alive and well. In his preface to *The Wretched of the Earth*, Jean-Paul Sartre couldn't find words strong enough for this colonized elite, whom he described as a "whitewashed" group of "false individuals who, "after a short stay in the mother country," become "walking lies [that] had nothing left to say to their brothers." Well, almost nothing has changed since the publication of Fanon's book in 1961. Certain stances evoke the well-known behavior of the "house negro," always so nervous about not being sufficiently loved by the Master. Once again, such attitudes are to be observed nowhere else on such a massive scale. To take only one example among thousands: never, under any pretext, would an American thinker ever qualify the September 11th attacks as a nonevent, and these were infinitely less costly in human lives than the genocide of the Tutsis. One of Yolande Mukagasana's books is entitled *N'aie pas peur de savoir* (Do Not Fear Knowing). This means that for the famous Rwandan survivor it is not enough to sympathize with the victims to make sense of the much-touted "Never Again": it is just as essential to know in detail the circumstances of the genocide and even the motivations of the *génocidaires* themselves. This refusal to face reality that Mukagasana dreads, even if it often takes refuge behind a noble alibi—"Let's not blame others for our own failures"—is above all the expression of a complete loss of self-esteem. In truth, it's not so much our eyes but rather our minds that turned away from the gigantic pile of cadavers on the Rwandan hills. And even if the difficulty of thinking the genocide came only from a feeling of shame, that would excuse nothing: to ignore your own history to that degree has more to do with a deficit of humanity than with a simple lack of information.

I was pretty much in this Afro-pessimistic state of mind when I arrived in Kigali, and felt ill at ease during those first few days. In my preceding novel, *Le Cavalier et son ombre* (*The Knight and His Shadow*), I had slipped in a few paragraphs about what I did not even dare call a genocide, without having ever set foot in Rwanda and without having had the faintest idea about what happened there between April and July 1994. Had I been hindered by ignorance alone? Not at all. Rather, at that time I was inclined to believe that the only chance for the world to be real was to be completely imaginary. I have, by the way, not entirely abandoned this idea. The novelist is not an historian, and by trying to come closer to reality, paradoxically, threatens to dissipate it in the way dreams fade away in the first light of morning, leaving us with the melancholic feeling that comes from knowing they will never return nor be retold. These wanderings in an obscure, uncertain and sometimes hostile universe bring the writer closer to the truth of beings and human societies. It is, moreover, to these bold innovations that Birago Diop urges us, in his version of another Wolof proverb: *When the memory goes to collect dead wood, she brings back the bundle that pleases her.*

All of this is of course true, but in the face of authentic human suffering, these aesthetic worries can seem completely trivial. Actually, if it is still so easy for us to forget Césaire's warning ("A screaming man is not a dancing bear"), this is because of our propensity to see in African tragedies not singular events but instead the successive and repeated sequences, ad infinitum, of a more widespread and ongoing cataclysm. In other words, each of these tragedies, far from existing in their own right and with their own particular complex political, economic, and cultural implications, are simply perceived as one of the many aftershocks of the same earthquake that has shaken the African continent without interruption since the dawn of time. With this in mind, Khadidja, the heroine in *The Knight and His Shadow*, could very well have substituted the word "Rwanda" with "Somalia," "Eritrea," "Liberia," or "Congo-Brazzaville" throughout the novel without ever leaving the impression that historical reference points had been blurred or that there was some kind of contradiction. Being a politically committed writer can come at the price of making such artificial and senseless connections. I thought I had relieved myself of my duty by allowing Khadidja to fulminate against the machete-slingers and shed tears for the victims of three months of carnage. Case closed and onward to the next ethnic cleansing, subject of my next book.

This is why I welcomed the offer to go to Kigali for a collective writing residency with more perplexity than enthusiasm. Having ultimately agreed to participate in the project through simple journalistic curiosity, my initial plan was to commit to a travel notebook, in absolute neutrality, a range of observations and possibly some impressions on a society that was quite foreign to me. I was not aware of this at the time, but I now realize that I hadn't been able to conceive of the Hundred Days of Slaughter in Rwanda other than as a tribal confrontation in which all the actors had, in equal measure, blood on their hands. That meant that before even knowing that a genocide had actually taken place, I was already one of those who subscribed to the theory of a Double Genocide! It can never be said enough how imperative it is for each of us to extricate Africa from herself before we have any chance of speaking about her rationally.

Thus, I did not want to leave the Land of a Thousand Hills with a work of fiction and, in a certain way, this promise was kept: *Murambi, The Book of Bones* grants much more importance to the facts brought by my interlocutors than to the sleights of hand often associated with experimental writing, which, if I may say so, was my trademark.

I completely changed my mind after being there for just one week.

The discussions with the survivors and the killers just like the visits to the sites of the genocide of the Tutsis taught me a lesson in history I was eager to share with my readers at all costs. I had just learned, to my great shame, what I should never had doubted, namely that in Rwanda, too, there were indeed victims and executioners. In *The Knight and His Shadow*, which partly focuses on the refugee camps of former Zaire, my mental confusion led me to involuntarily grant more attention to the *génocidaires* who, in fact, were continuing to spread terror in Mugunga and Uvira. While the chiefs of these camps had just perpetrated the last genocide of the 20th century, I depicted them, with quavering pen, as innocent people who had escaped from killers and devoted all their time to supporting, with nobility of soul, the widow and the orphan.

I soon understood that the best way to avoid repeating such a serious misunderstanding was by respecting the witness statements collected during our stay in Rwanda while placing them in the Rwandan historical context. It was not therefore a matter of writing a book on an "African genocide"—an expression which in any case is too vague to deserve, I was starting to realize, the least interest—but, very concretely, a book on the genocide of the Tutsis in Rwanda.

I must add that in spite of this concern for factual precision, *Murambi, The Book of Bones* remains a novel to the extent that it tells the tumult of a tragic history and through diverse, individual trajectories, one author's subjectivity. Indeed, if Rwanda had ever been this peaceful, luminous place where the God Imana came to rest after every sunset, it had ceased to be so for a long time by 1998: death continued to lurk everywhere, the stench of decomposing corpses still took you by the throat, and the survivors had still not emerged from their long state of silent stupefaction. To be at every instant driven back a little deeper into the darkness lessens your desire to keep a travel journal. You just don't take notes beside a mass grave. My commitment to accurately representing the experiences of my interlocutors did not waiver, but I relinquished the scientist's neutrality. It was no longer a question of coldly collecting the facts but of listening to the stories of destroyed men and women and of giving them a voice.

It was much easier to dream of this generous "writing project" than to implement it and it literally took weeks for me to know exactly what to do with what I had seen and heard. Even choosing the form of a novel, which had always been so natural to me, did not seem obvious. For example, I hesitated between writing a vengeful pamphlet on the criminal flippancy of the UN in Rwanda and a play, traces of which are, by the way, to be found in the final text. The people we were dealing with had been transfigured by their ordeal. They hardly looked like ordinary human beings and their stories were so exceptional that every day the action of my novel developed around a different plot than the one I had in mind the day before. I remember having heard, for example, in the company of Monique Ilboudo, the story of the distressing passionate love between a young woman and her savior, a soldier who would end up half-crazed. I even considered for some time making this story, a perfect foreshadowing of postgenocide Rwanda, the subject of my book. It ended being recounted in *Murekatete* by the one and only Monique. It was also in her company that I attended the interrogation of a *génocidaire* in a police station. The man, who denied nothing, took refuge behind the habitual "I acted under orders from the burgomaster." He had lost both ears during a particularly violent arrest and this had rendered him so grotesque and pitiful that the scene was unbearable. Why not, I asked myself, connect the fate of this poor devil with that of Bagosora, Nahimana, or one of the other alleged masterminds behind the genocide that had been exfiltrated from Rwanda by the French military Operation Turquoise? I abandoned this idea as well. But with each new day, chance continued to furnish the text-to-be with subtle hints. Here is one example among many: One Sunday morning, we were attending an exhumation ceremony of the remains of victims on Nyanza hill. We were lost in the crowd that was coming and going. Two women passed close to me and I heard one tell her companion, "This is where our Cornelius was killed." I did not yet know which novel I would write, but at that moment I thought that no matter what happened, the main character would be named Cornelius. Having said this, it was during an encounter between our group and the survivors' association, "Pro-Femmes/Twese Hamwe," that I was most deeply impressed and moved. On that day, one of the survivors calmly told us why her anger remained unabated: "Since 1959," she declared, "every time there is a massacre, the same man, one of our neighbors, comes over to our house with his sons to kill whoever is inside. In 1994, they came back and I was the only one to escape, I have no relatives left in the world. The man was thrown in prison after the genocide, but then the government released him on account of his old age. Now, every morning on my way to work, I see him sitting on the stoop of his house and he follows me with his eyes until I disappear around the street corner." When the young woman reached the end of her statement, her voice seemed just as serene but you could tell that recalling this memory had awoken a cold anger, a deep-seated hatred, in her heart, and enunciating her words carefully, she shot a slightly wild-eyed look, her finger pointed at her chest: "And they want *me* to forgive. . . ?" This last question seemed directed at herself more than the audience. It was the ideal story, bringing face to face, from one massacre to the next, perpetrators and victims who found themselves, on top of everything, longstanding neighbors. If it only inspired one chapter of my book—the conversation between Faustin Gasana and his father—this is because many other stories had also caught my attention and I wanted to find a way to integrate all of them, in one way or another, into *Murambi, The Book of Bones*. The book's fragmented structure can be explained, moreover, by this desire to showcase or approach a myriad of individual destinies during the genocide. Having come to Rwanda "by duty of memory," I was determined not to abandon anyone on the side of the road. I discovered, on the way, something that struck me as fundamental: if a genocide as spectacular as that of the Tutsis in Rwanda involves screaming masses of men and women caught in the trap of a nameless, collective panic, each person only hears in this formidable upheaval the beating of his own heart, in sudden and horrible proximity with his own death. I also had to find a way to convey the solitude of people abandoned to their fate, a solitude sometimes even more terrifying than the bloody chaos surrounding them. If I definitively chose the story that you just read, this is because I owe another equally essential lesson to Rwanda: the crime of genocide is committed by the fathers but it is atoned for by the sons.

As writers we were all, of course, exposed to the same novelistic temptations. That's why most of the texts mention Theresa Mukandori, so savagely tortured in Nyamata, and one of the central figures in Koulsy Lamko's *La Phalène des collines* (*The Moth of the Hills*). But luckily, the goal of the project was not the composition of a collective work. If that had been the case, we most likely would have never managed to write so much as the first line, because the creation of a novel is anything but a team effort. So much so that very quickly each of us spontaneously traced our personal paths in Kigali. These niches we carved out in our schedule, that we later referred to as our own "private beaches," ended up replacing, with the consent of the organizers, all of the group activities.

It was while evolving in solitary that I crossed paths with two exceptional individuals, Jeanne K. and the old Apollinaire. *Murambi, The Book of Bones* owes much more to our hours of conversation, in a nearly deserted house—in Kimihurura, if my memory serves me right—than to the reading I did for my research or to the documentaries I watched that were left at our disposal. Jeanne and Apollinaire served as my models for the characters Jessica and Siméon and I am grateful to them for having allowed me to catch sight of that little glimmer of hope, without which, it seems, no novel could be written.

Because we all experienced Rwanda in such disparate ways, the experience itself impacted us differently. The most striking case is that of Koulsy Lamko. He was supposed to visit Rwanda from July to September 1998 like the rest of us, but he ended up staying on until 2002. The Chadian author had no idea how long he would live in Rwanda, nor what precisely he would do there, or for that matter how he would end up making a decision that would have such lasting personal consequences. He just said to himself after eight weeks of being there: "I cannot come to this country, see all of this abomination, then write a book and return to my everyday business as if it were nothing." Despite the institutional and moral support of Rwandan friends, such as Doctor Émile Rwamasirabo, rector at the time of the National University of Rwanda in Butare, and his wife Alice Karekezi, a legal expert and social activist, those four years were not always easy. Koulsy Lamko devoted them to cultivating to the best of his ability the creative potential of the youth of Butare, in particular in the theatrical domain, which actually happens to be his academic specialty. From this unexpected extension of "Rwanda: Writing by Duty of Memory" initiative, the Centre universitaire des Arts (University Centre for the Arts) was established in September 1999, and has been officially integrated into the curriculum of students in arts and letters in Butare since 2001. And it most certainly was not a coincidence that Professor Jean-Marie Kayishema agreed to direct it. An academic and playwright himself, Kayishema is among those who view the deficit of symbolic representation in Rwandan society—brutally deprived of its spiritual bearings by a fundamentalist brand of evangelization—as one of the underlying causes of the genocide. Based on this assessment, numerous artistic activities have unfolded over the years under the umbrella of the Centre for Arts and Drama. "Ingoma Nshiye," an all-women drumming group of about twenty—the number can rise to about one hundred for some performances—was created thanks to this structure. Incidentally, this represents a major rupture with the old guard since formerly in Rwanda only men were allowed to play the drum.

And that's not all, because from Mexico where he's lived for several years, Koulsy Lamko coordinated—with Palmira Telesforo Cruz and myself—a collective work dedicated to our residency in 1998. Published in January 2009 under the title *Genocidio de los Tutsis de Ruanda: la memoria en camino* (*Genocide of the Tutsis of Rwanda: Memory on the Road*), it is the only resource on this subject available in Spanish. The utility and urgency of this work are undeniable, reconnecting as it does South America and Africa whose people, equally afflicted by a barbarous conquest, have abandoned their tradition of dialogue, especially since the end of the Cold War. Two other writers from our group—Abdourahman Waberi and Véronique Tadjo—contributed to *Genocidio de los Tutsis de Ruanda: la memoria en camino*. Yet another piece of evidence, if one was needed, of the near-impossibility of emerging from the Rwandan experience unscathed.

In short, Koulsy Lamko gave an original response to the nagging question of the legitimacy of fictionalizing genocide—a question that the Kigali authorities were the first to ask us, however indirectly: "Yes, one can write a novel about the genocide of the Tutsis, but as long as one isn't confined to only that."

The works of Josias Semujanga, Yolande Mukagasana, and Benjamin Tsehene, among others, helped me to better understand the Rwandan tragedy at the time when I was writing my own. That said, the residents of Nyamirambo had been among the first non-Rwandans to work on the genocide of the Tutsis. At the time, in fact, cinema, theater, choreography, the fine arts, and literature had not yet made genocide one of their favorite subjects.

Nevertheless, the situation has changed significantly since the day when we took up quarters at *La Mise*. Millions of people have by now seen the films *Sometimes in April* or *Hotel Rwanda*, as well as the numerous documentaries and fictional films dedicated to the genocide of the Tutsis: if *Rwanda 94* by Groupov is a particularly ambitious and successful spectacle, the plays inspired by this theme are today too numerous for any of us to count; artists such as Bruce Clarke and Kofi Setordji focused on the One Hundred Days of Slaughter in Rwanda and *Fagaala*, by the choreographers Germaine Acogny and Kota Yamasaki, is an adaptation of *Murambi, The Book of Bones*. After having covered the tragedy, journalists such as Philip Gourevitch, Jean-François Dupaquier, Patrick de Saint-Exupéry, and Colette Braeckman returned to it in works that admirably complement those written by professional historians. But the most important component of the work has been, and continues to be done, by Rwandans themselves who often were not able to speak out until much later, following a relatively long period of mourning. This was the case, to name a few, of Annick Kayitesi, Révérien Rurangwa, Scholastique Mukasonga, and Esther Muyawayo.

One only has to compare the very first celebrations of the anniversary of the genocide with those of today to gauge the improved understanding there is of its mechanisms as well as the fact that there is now infinitely more compassion for the victims. This is owed in large part to the wealth of scholarly and literary production. Still, the almost complete absence of African intellectuals in all the bibliographies related to the genocide remains shocking. This state of affairs may be partially explained by the fact that it is extremely difficult for Africans to get published in Africa or elsewhere. But this situation is not unique to Rwanda, and one finds a similar silence when it comes to coverage of other conflicts, and only rarely do journalists and scholars working in

Africa feel the obligation to help their fellow citizens to know *precisely* what happened at a given time and in a particular place. For example, how many among us, even the most educated, are able to explain, even in the vaguest terms, what was at stake in the civil wars in Liberia, Congo-Brazzaville or Sierra Leone? In Monrovia and Freetown, warlords chopped off hands and heads, and then one day peace returned and that was the last we heard of that. . . . The same occurred in Rwanda, where politicians, admittedly with limited intelligence, told their followers: "Grab your machetes, and head for the hills and into the streets and kill all our enemies, every last one of them, just make sure they suffer a thousand deaths before dying!" and, aside from the survivors and a handful of writers from neighboring countries, all the available information—at times precious, often biased—comes from scholars, political activists, humanitarians, and western journalists. This is a serious anomaly and the real merit of "Rwanda: Writing by Duty of Memory" has been to make some African voices heard far from the Great Lakes Region.

Every talk that I have given about *Murambi, The Book of Bones* has given me the opportunity to verify the extent to which any attempt at extermination always resonates with other historical experiences with which, a priori, there is no special relationship. In my case, the genocide of the Tutsis recalled a certain colonial past. So the most obvious step for me was to focus on France's role in Rwandan genocide and *Négrophobie*, a book I cowrote with Odile Tobner and François-Xavier Verschave, therefore stands as the logical continuation of the Rwandan adventure. The work was born from the premise that everyday racism, a ferment of France's colonial policies, has remained a half-century after our so-called Independences at the heart of its African foreign policy. The situation is of course even more serious than people may think, and the cases of Madagascar, of the Bamileke region in Cameroon, or of Algeria serve to highlight how France committed more massacres in its multiple attempts to stay on in Africa than they had in the process of conquering it. And during the Cold War, every time they had the opportunity to decolonize without granting freedom, they seized it, immediately placing their lackeys at the helm of new states, and subsequently by protecting them through armed intervention each time they were confronted with a popular uprising. The most striking aspect of this is how this behavior never prevented them from maintaining their claim to being "the birthplace of human rights." Has this been the source of even the slightest embarrassment? Not in the least. In a recent documentary, Jacques Foccart and a few key players in his network are shown explaining to the public at large, in all serenity, how they went about implementing the neocolonial infrastructure of *Françafrique*. In the twilight of their lives, these aging civil servants, a smile on their lips and a glass of cognac in hand, revisit fifty years of dirty tricks. Yes, Moumié, he wasn't too bad at first but he turned into a smart ass, so I had him poisoned in Geneva by some guy posing as a journalist. Guinea? I poured billions of fake bank bills into the country to destabilize Sékou Touré and, I don't want to brag, but the operation was a smashing success. The list goes on: tailor-made military coups, all-out military interventions, the pillage by Elf of the oil resources of Gabon and the Congo in order to guarantee, in the Gaullist scheme of things, France's autonomy from the two great powers of the era. Gabon and the Congo as the guarantors of France's independence: now isn't that lovely? These heirs of the Enlightenment we have to listen to in this film have so little remorse that one is hard pressed to believe that they are in fact giving an account of the systematic, and extremely costly in terms of human life, destruction of poor countries.

And yet they were not saying anything that the French hadn't already read or heard. In actuality, the very fact that they were so quick to confess just confirms their awareness of the fact that their supposedly secret actions had long been an open secret. And if they did not fear being viewed negatively by their neighbors, this is because the average French person's prejudices about Africa have not lessened over the years. In the end, whatever harm they had done to this continent didn't really matter a whole lot.

This certainty that they can do whatever they want to their subjects in their African *pré-carré* is why France is today lost to Rwanda.

For having behaved in Rwanda as they had previously in Chad or in Cameroon, France must now reckon with the shameful accusation of complicity in the genocide and with the *Hutu Power*. The words of former President François Mitterrand ("In such countries, a genocide doesn't really matter") rely on an idea as old as *Françafrique* itself, namely that Africa's bad reputation will always allow them, in case of necessity, to play on the negrophobic reflexes of public opinion. Jean d'Ormesson feared no backlash when he insulted in the *Figaro Littéraire* magazine the victims of a genocide in which he only saw, after a short trip to Rwanda in June 1994, "grandiose massacres in sublime landscapes." "A genocide that doesn't really matter"? "Grandiose massacres"? It is beyond me how, in this day and age, one can make such repugnant remarks.

The memory of a genocide is a paradoxical memory, and the more time passes, the less we forget and, in April 1998, Jacques Julliard warned in his column in the *Nouvel Observateur*: "One day, the question of France's responsibility will be raised, François Mitterrand having been President of the Republic, in the genocide of the Tutsis in Rwanda in 1994. France did not commit the crime, but it put weapons in the hands of future killers who did not hide their intentions." Such a trial has yet to be held, and even if Mitterrand continues to be perceived as a good-hearted humanist, mindsets in France regarding Rwanda have evolved considerably since the days when, practically alone and against everyone, Mehdi Bâ, Patrick de Saint-Exupéry, and François-Xavier Verschave stood outraged by Paris's support for the murderous killers in Kigali. The work of various commissions and that of historians, along with a number of hearings conducted by the International Criminal Court, have contributed to these changes by making all the necessary information available. Thanks to this abundant documentation that has been mined by specialists, the debate on the French state's complicity in the genocide has shifted from the terrain of pure speculation toward that of *facts*. Unexpectedly, Paris found itself obliged to abandon its habitual position and defense strategy. Almost overnight, it became impossible to play the false innocent, as Mitterrand had at the eighteenth Franco-

African summit held in Biarritz in November 1994: "What can France really be expected to do when African chiefs decide to settle their quarrels with machetes?" The accusations became so specific that they were obliged to respond to them *point by point*. Likewise, they also had to justify how, among other things and in violation of the UN embargo, deliveries of arms to the Rwandan government had been ongoing at the same very moment when the country was littered with hundreds of thousands of cadavers; inquiring minds also wanted to know why the same *génocidaire* government had been constituted at the beginning of April 1994 on the premises of the French Embassy in Kigali, under the supervision of then French Ambassador Jean-Michel Marlaud. The French army's role in training the killer militias also elicited legitimate questions.

Paris' response to these grievances have been singularly unconvincing, and even if it has not fundamentally changed anything for French citizens, at least they know that their country was an important actor in the last genocide of the 20th century. That is no small achievement. Genocide is after all the ultimate crime and it is more than dishonorable to be associated with those who planned and carried out the extermination of the Tutsis in Rwanda.

This is certainly the reason why so many French academics and politicians came out and sought to deny this genocide in myriad ways. Where there's smoke, there's fire, and this stubborn attitude against a small country in which France had only attained a firm foothold in 1973 speaks for itself. We must not forget moreover that one of the distinctive features of the genocide of the Tutsis was that it was the object of a sort of universal denial at the same time that it was being perpetrated. Certain "special" advisors to the Elysée Palace did not wait for the end of the genocide to encourage the media to present Paul Kagame as the leader of a kind of "Black Khmers." This bold semantic gamble failed but this did not put an end to attempts at demonizing the Rwandan president. This was done by equal parts omission and defamation. This is how news of Rwandan economic growth, which Abdourahman

Waberi brought to light in a special issue of *Courrier international*, was systematically ignored. What these economic indicators revealed were a country's capacity for resilience, a country confident enough in itself to abolish the death penalty on July 25, 2007. No one talked about that either. However, such a measure, important anywhere in our world, had a particularly strong symbolic value in Rwanda.

Kagame could hardly be blamed for the butchery orchestrated by *Hutu Power*, so instead he was accused of having played a part in provoking Bagosora and his supporters by making an attempt on the life of Juvénal Habyarimana. . . . That was the avenue pursued by Judge Jean-Louis Bruguière when he indicted Kagame and his associates. We believed at the beginning he was there to serve justice, but in reality he was merely there to serve the interests of his country. Indeed, *WikiLeaks* revealed that his arrest warrant itself had been concocted in concert with the Élysée Palace during Chirac's presidency. . . . In any case, the affair had lost all momentum well before the revelations, as all the witnesses cobbled together by Bruguière withdrew their testimony one after the other, as reported by the daily newspapers *Libération* and *Le Monde* at the end of 2006. The objective of intimidating Kagame and keeping him under "house arrest" in his own country proved to be totally ineffective and he only increased his travel during those months. Finally, it was President Nicolas Sarkozy himself who went to Kigali on February 25, 2010. Aside from the remorse that he half-heartedly expressed, this brief visit by the French president to Rwandan soil was, in itself, a first-class burial for Bruguière's dossier. After all, one is not supposed to compromise oneself with a pariah president, especially after he broke all diplomatic relations with your country and showed increasing gestures of defiance over the years.

The UN report on the Congo also failed to give the theory of a Double Genocide the second wind some had hoped for. For this to happen, its authors would have had to respond to a very straightforward question, which they only briefly alluded to: why had the RPF gone to so much trouble to repatriate Hutu refugees from the

Congo to Rwanda, where today they constitute the majority of the population? As numerous observers have highlighted, this is not how you treat the people you want to exterminate.

In the end, it doesn't really matter whether one likes Kagame or not. We are talking about the genocide of the Tutsis, and it was the RPF who ended it. And it would be absurd to expect the Rwandan people to forget about it from one day to the next under the pretext that it is time to turn the page. It is reported that during their private meeting on the sidelines of a summit in Lisbon in 2007, Sarkozy warned Kagame that "for sake of France's honor," the accusation of complicity in the genocide would not be tolerated. To which the Rwandan leader supposedly responded in a very calm tone: "Mr. President, do you know of an honorless country?" This exchange illustrates not only on which side the moral superiority lies, it is also a sign of a new era. For France, which has never needed to deny anything regarding its African policies, the necessity to unbridle its "intellectual operatives" in order to elaborate a discourse denying genocide is, in itself, a humiliation.

It is difficult to tell what sort of future is in store for Kagame's project for Rwanda, but we would be wrong to underestimate his disdain and that of a growing number of African leaders for countries that persist in talking down to them. No one is awestruck by Europe anymore and, to be honest, nowhere in the world is its hegemony still obvious. It no longer has virtually unlimited access to the resources of the nations of South America and Asia, and if Africa remains its last reservoir for raw materials—the only security it has in old age—there is reason to believe that the situation could change more rapidly than we imagine.

None of that was on my mind when I embarked, almost twenty years ago now, on an Ethiopian Airlines flight for Kigali. I went to Rwanda to write a novel and history caught up with me. The sudden appearance of several authors in the same country to carve out their fables, in the course of two months, upon its battered body, was not only an unprecedented literary experiment, it was also the opportunity to take the kind of action every artist secretly dreams about. Even though creators often disdain politicians, for the most part they envy their energy and their capacity to directly influence the lives of their fellow citizens. The prospect of immersing oneself in the real in such a powerful way had never been presented to us prior to the "Rwanda: Writing by Duty of Memory" project and we all welcomed the occasion to produce, in the literal sense of the term, a *meaningful work*.

Nostalgia is mingled, of course, in what follows.

On the 10th anniversary of the creation of the University Center for the Arts, in February 2010, we decided, Koulsy Lamko and myself, to make a trip back to *La Mise Hôtel*. Koulsy wanted to interview me for *Feeding Roots*, the documentary on Rwanda that he was filming at the time, and for this recording no place seemed more appropriate than our old "base" in Kigali. Only, you see: Speciose, the owner with the bright and cheerful eyes, who used to lean on the counter in the reception area, was nowhere to be found. In fact, the counter itself was gone because the hotel in Nyamirambo quite simply no longer existed. Our rooms on the second floor had been converted into offices and the restaurant-bar on the first floor was now a hair salon. The landlady, a Congolese woman from Kinshasa was kind enough to allow us to take pictures but this *Mise Hôtel* certainly was not the one we had known. There were almost grounds to feel betrayed. But were we still the same, Koulsy and I? Certainly not. Our time spent together in this place a decade earlier had made of us the best of friends but also completely changed us. An idea unexpectedly came to my mind that day: if we ever dared repeat the project "Rwanda: Writing by Duty of Memory," our books would certainly have nothing in common with those that were published at the end of the residency in 1998. I guess that mine would be missing the desire, once so strong, to make the reader feel the shock and the fright that came with the discovery of a horror defying imagination, both literally and figuratively. The adventure, however, remains irreplaceable, not so much for literary reasons but because the books themselves that came of it contributed to doing justice, in their own modest way, to the victims of the genocide.

I wanted to add an afterword to this new edition of *Murambi, The Book of Bones* in order to recall all of this. I also wanted to remain, by this means, in dialogue with readers who still write to me all these years after the first publication of the novel. One of these letters, which I received in November 2010 from Giusy M., a Romanian academic, demonstrates that this time, at least, our work had not been in vain: "For years," she admits, "I suffered enormously from what happened in Rwanda, yet without ever being able to find anything in common with all those perpetrators and victims, who somehow all became confused. For me, this was all happening in a distant and unfamiliar world, in a world that was completely alien to me. Through my readings of works of fiction about the genocide, I gradually started to feel as close to the people there as I did to my next door neighbors, and now I realize that nothing, absolutely nothing, makes me any different from them. I am them and they are me, and that's all there is to it."

Of course we still have a long way to go before everyone is able to take in the measure of the tragedy of 1994, but when a reader, far from Rwanda, rehumanizes the victims in this way by identifying with them, it is possible to speak of a reassuring victory against the killers. The duty of memory is first and foremost a way of opposing a life project to that of annihilation offered by the *génocidaires*, and the novelist has a say in this. In any case, there is no point saddling the writer with the ambition to move mountains with his dreams alone. When it comes down to it, writers are usually more humble than that and just knowing that they were able to do "a little good" is often enough to make them happy.

Translated by Cristina Politano and Dominic Thomas